THE MIDLIFE LADY'S GUIDE TO A BAD HOROSCOPE

POWERS OF THE ZODIAC - PREQUEL NOVELLA

KATE KARYUS QUINN   DEMITRIA LUNETTA

MARLEY LYNN

For the families we're born with...and the ones we find along the way.

Visit MarleyLynn.com to sign up for the Mythverse Newsletter and you'll receive **FREE SHORT STORIES**—all set in the Mythverse!

1

Maddie

I know that I'm not the first bride to be left standing at the altar with no groom in sight. It's almost a cliché — one that's always played for laughs—and usually gets them.

I'm not laughing.

But I am *smiling*, because I am Madison Thorne and Madison Thorne is always smiling. You can see it in my Facebook posts with my beautiful family, my Instagram pics with my latest to-die-for crafting idea, and in the Pinterest board of ideas I made for this special day.

Except I had always imagined that my husband would be next to me.

Okay, maybe I *am* laughing. It's a slightly hysterical giggle—there's a limit to grace under pressure. Because here's the thing: while a bride can get stood up on her wedding day by a groom with cold feet...how many women deal with a no-show husband for a vow *renewal* ceremony?

I give the minister a piece of my strained smile. We're

not regular churchgoers, really, just Christmas and Easter with the family. But this minister married us twenty-five years ago and I thought it would be nice to have him perform our vow renewal, even though there's nothing religious about it. We're not even having our ceremony in a church. We're in a beautiful forest—my idea—and the spring breeze rushing past me is comforting.

Well, kind of.

About twelve years ago a cataclysmic event sent shock waves through the entire world. Natural disasters erupted everywhere, food chain supplies were broken, and it kind of felt like the apocalypse for a little bit. But the biggest shock by far was that it turned out all of the paranormal creatures we'd thought were myths were actually quite real. Vampires, werewolves, pixies, and all kinds of bizarre creatures came out of the woodwork, and it took some time for humans to adapt to the new normal.

Things were a bit hairy for a while. Some of the supes made gangs, claimed territory, and then moved on to terrorizing everyone in the vicinity. We were lucky to live in a neighborhood that was spared from the worst of it. But the church we were married in was not so fortunate. Apparently some fae fire balls went astray when they were fighting a gang of vampires. The interior of the church went up in flames, leaving only the brick shell standing. Last I heard a pack of harpy meth-heads are squatting there.

Honestly, I'm not too broken up about not being able to recreate the "I dos" we exchanged inside that dark old building. In my memories of that day, I recall feeling trapped and boxed in. I was young and powerless. It never occurred to me that I could have a say in my own destiny. Of course, it all worked out. But still, it feels good to be the one steering the ship this time.

If only I could've steered Bert's ship too, maybe he would be here right now.

With that thought, I glance over my shoulder.

Everyone I know is here...minus my husband. My parents, my kids, friends, family. And they're all looking at me with various levels of pity in their eyes. Well, no, actually, my youngest boy, Oliver, hasn't looked up from his phone. The signal out here isn't great, but I guess he doesn't need it for that shooting game he loves.

Love. Yeah. My monosyllabic son definitely loves his computer games. It's the only topic where I can get more than one-word answers from him. Once Ollie was so excited about a new skin he bought, he waxed poetic about it for a full ten minutes. I had no idea what he was talking about, but I feigned enthusiasm for his sake—after first Googling to figure out what a skin was, and hoping that my youngest wasn't wandering into some weird internet sex thing.

'Cause that's love too. Isn't it?

You take an interest in the things your loved one cares about. It's a form of showing up, even if in this instance it was only me murmuring, "Oooh," "Wow," and "Yeah, of course you should get the beheading emote."

My husband Bert is terrible at showing up in these small ways. Instead, he's the master of the grand gesture. Like a wedding renewal ceremony in front of all our friends and family.

That's how I know this is not a case of cold feet. Bert and I have been married for twenty-five years. And this whole renewal thing was his idea. He'd wanted to give me the ceremony in the woods that I'd always dreamed about—instead of the stuffy church wedding that my parents provided when I was eighteen and had a bun in the oven.

The thought of the reception dinner at the ancient firemen's hall with three hundred of our not-so-closest friends and relatives still makes me cringe. It had sticky floors and reeked of old booze and stale beer. It didn't help that I was nauseous the whole time and trying desperately to suck in my baby bump. I'd smiled through it all, though.

So here we are, in a clearing that the park service rents out for events. I had to work hard to not make it look like a summer camp pow-wow. I cleaned out the fire pit, raked all of the leaves and sticks for at least half an acre, and set up soft lighting. White Christmas lights were in the discount bin and they look lovely wound around the trees, and if a few pixies are hovering around them it just adds to the ambience. I know that particular types of supe—what people call the supernaturals—are attracted to lights, so the Christmas bulbs are doing double duty.

I even put mosquito lures in the forest in a one-mile radius so all annoying bugs would be drawn to them and leave our guests alone. As usual, I've thought of everything.

There was no sound system so I rented a generator and got the DJ set up ahead of time, all the while praying that it wouldn't rain. I got a great deal on renting a few hundred white chairs from the church, but they were a bit dingy so I got them to knock off the price if I painted them all. I even hand-stenciled a small lily onto the backrest of each one, adding a nice floral touch that can also be religious for when the chairs go back to their rightful owners.

I didn't want to spend the money on catering so I cooked everything myself, including three hundred mini cakes. Each one was hand frosted by yours truly with a heart and *Maddie & Bert* lovingly written in pink buttercream. I think I gave myself carpal tunnel—either that or I am clutching this bouquet way too hard. I force myself to relax and hope that the tension from my hands didn't go up into my smile. It needs to look natural, just like everything else out here. Everything for my perfect day.

It was worth all the work. I came in way under budget. Not that Bert gave me one. He actually specifically told me not to pinch pennies. But Bert doesn't balance the checkbook. I do. And right now...things are tight. I know it'll all turn out okay, somehow it always does. Just when it seems like we won't be able to pay the mortgage, Bert returns from Southern France—or some other equally exotic destination—with a new antique that he sells for an amount big enough to make all our dreams come true...for a while at least.

I could make one of those checks last a lifetime. But Bert's dreams are too big. And expensive. He says that's why we make a perfect team. His head is in the clouds while my feet are on the ground. And he's right; we've gone through twenty-five years this way. It's just that sometimes...

With a sigh, I lift my head to the sky, it's clear and the full moon hangs low, visible even though night is hours away. Someone was telling me something about this moon...it was a blood moon or something. I can't remember. Maybe tonight after the guests leave and it's just me and Bert we can turn off all the lights and lay under the night sky to stargaze...and then maybe direct our attention elsewhere.

Beside me, the minister clears his throat. The last twenty-five years haven't been kind to him; he needs a cane to stay upright and is looking deeply uncomfortable. "It's been thirty-five minutes..." he tells me. His tone is apologetic, but there's an edge that wasn't in his voice when we first realized that Bert was missing. Then he said, "Renewal ceremonies are such joyous occasions. Like so many of the best things in life, they're worth waiting for." I guess, like everyone, the minister has limits.

"Just five more minutes," I say. The same as I've said six times now. I hope my smile still looks genuine, and I'm not showing too many teeth. Even if I did have them whitened just for the occasion.

His lips compress, but then he nods. I know that I won't get another five minutes after this. If Bert doesn't show soon this minister will be walking—or, em, shuffling—away.

Darn it, Bert!

I smooth down my dress—a beautiful retro piece from the seventies that I found at a garage sale while looking for the vintage clothing shop—and sigh once more.

My Bert. I've told him so many times that he packs his days too full. He's a man who is hungry for life. He wants to experience everything. It's what I love about him. But also, after twenty plus years, it's what leads to most of my frustrations with him. He's never on time, dashing in at the last possible minute for parent-teacher conferences. Or showing up fashionably late to parties being thrown in our own backyard. Once he was in charge of bringing the welcome bags, and showed up just in time to give them to guests as they were leaving.

And it's not that he forgets. It's always, "I'm sorry baby, I got hung up..."

He's a businessman. Always making deals, meeting new people, cementing old friendships, and then selling something to them. And he financially supports our family—as he reminds me more often than is altogether necessary. There's a little flare of anger in my stomach at the thought, and I have to work hard to keep my smile in place. The minister clears his throat and I know it's time to get this party started—without the groom.

Unlike the first time around, this is *my day*. And nothing —not even my husband—is going to ruin it for me.

I turn to face my family and friends. "We all know Bert; he probably spotted a piece of artwork in the airport that is worth more than anyone ever thought, and is currently haggling with the art director—who will be his new best friend after some drinks. So let's go ahead and celebrate, and we can do the ceremony later!" I say, with a huge smile.

There is a collective sigh of relief. I make sure the minister gets a chair so he can rest, give a wave to the DJ to let him know to start spinning, and put the fairy lights on twinkle mode, which brings in a few more pixies and makes for a festive atmosphere. I assure everyone that I'm fine; it's just an unexpected delay. I move from group to group, smiling like my life depends on it.

I read once that a scientific study showed that the physical act of smiling can actually help lift a person's mood. Now, though, I have to wonder exactly how they knew this. I'd lie through my upturned lips that this is a perfect day and that my every smile only increases my joy. And if they called me on it, I'd only smile harder.

"Mom, are you okay?" my oldest, Nathan, asks. How am I old enough to have a twenty-four-year old child?! He's already in grad school. An actual adult. I am old enough to have three adult children. Even number four, the baby, is now in high school! Nathan sees the stricken look on my face and misunderstands—he thinks I'm upset with his father. And of course I'm not. Of course I'm not mad at Bert. Of course not.

"Yes, you know your father," I say with a wave of my hand.

"He doesn't deserve you," he mumbles. "He takes you for granted." My heart twists for my little boy, even if he is all grown up now. Once he worshipped the ground Bert walked on. But too many years of missed baseball games, debate finals, and even his college graduation has put a strain on their relationship. I make a note to have Bert invite him for a guy's night out. They'll have some drinks together and Bert will smooth things over until Nathan forgets all about those old hurts. Well...mostly.

"Marriage is work," I tell him, giving his arm a little squeeze. "You'll understand one day."

"Sure. Mom, get some food," he says. But I probably won't. There's a feeling in my stomach that doesn't mix well with food. Disappointment. My face still apparently isn't doing a great job of conveying absolute joy, because Nathan's glower deepens.

I decide it's time to change the subject. "Do you know who that man is over there?" I point to a tall dark-haired man who slipped into the party late. Irrationally, I'm a bit annoyed at this stranger—not for crashing my party, but for giving me a moment's hope that Bert had finally arrived.

Nathan frowns. "I saw Aunt Stephy hanging on him earlier..." he says.

"Oh, okay," I say, since that pretty much answers it all.

My younger sister Stephanie is a triple divorcée on the hunt for number four. Which is fine. To each their own. I'm not here to judge her choices. But it's a bit annoying that she refuses to extend the same courtesy to me. She's made it very clear that she thinks this whole vow renewal ceremony is lame and cheesy and—worst of all—smug.

Well, I bet she's loving how things turned out. There's nothing to be smug about now.

Again, Nathan must see something of what I'm thinking, because he curls his hands into fists. "When Dad shows up I'm going to..."

"You won't do anything," I cut him off. "You won't ruin the party."

"Dad already did that," he shoots back, but he won't cause a fuss. He knows I would hate that. Any type of confrontation is absolutely not my thing. Bert likes to talk about how we never fight. Ever. He does a whole little bit about it when we meet new people.

"This is my wife, Maddie," he says, a twinkle in his eyes. "I know the name paired with that wild curly hair of hers makes her look like a lady with a temper. But believe it or not, we've never had a single fight. And it's not because I'm a perfect saint either. Or no, I could *tempt* a saint." He pauses here for knowing laughter from those familiar with him—and almost everyone is. Then he continues, "But my Maddie here, she never gets mad."

Then it's my turn to give the punchline, "I never get mad, but someday I might get even."

Every single time Bert reacts like it's his first time hearing it. His eyes pop wide and he startles back, a hand to his heart. "Uh-oh," he cries as the laughter around us grows louder. "I better watch myself then!'

I always laugh along. But I have to say, I've noticed that he never joins in. Instead, he smiles and takes a drink, always surveying those around us to make sure he's doing his job of making everyone like him. Sometimes when I see him reading the room like that it sends a chill up my spine...and not always a good one. He always knows how to get exactly the right reaction out of people, and how to get what he wants from them. Lord knows he's got me. Smiling, Maddie "Never Mad" Thorne.

But really this might be the last straw. Maybe this time I won't shove my feelings down. Maybe this time I'll curse him out and threaten to...

I don't know what I'd do. I've put so much work into being perfectly nice that I don't even know how to get angry. And it's not like I could ever throw something at Bert, stamp my foot and demand an apology—I've never had to. He always walks in the door with the right words, and I can't resist a man who isn't afraid to say he's sorry.

I've loved Robert Thorne for as long as I can remember.

"Mom!" the twins call to me. "Come dance!"

I plaster on a smile and go to them. They are a perfectly adorable pair, with matching faces that somehow look great on both a boy and a girl. In family pictures we always look fantastic, even if Bert is sometimes a little flushed from running into the studio fifteen minutes behind schedule.

The music is lovely as it bounces off the trees and flows through the evening air, the pixies bobbing up and down along with it. It's getting darker, and we'll have to pay some attention to make sure there aren't any harpies or vampires lurking in the higher branches of the trees, but the park service does a pretty good job of keeping public areas free of some of the more violent supes. In fact, I had raided the cash register at my vintage clothing store to slip the rangers a few extra twenties to keep them on the party perimeter after sunset, just in case.

I had a plan, and I wasn't going to let anything ruin my perfect night.

But I didn't plan on my husband being a no-show.

2

—————

Helena

I have exactly thirty-five minutes between meetings so I put my foot on the gas and drive like my life depends on it. Or maybe just my sanity. Although I can't afford to lose that either. When you are a lady lawyer, being sane is a must.

"Ms. McCready," my secretary, Joel's, voice, comes from the speaker. "Your two o'clock wants to move to four but you have a Zoom scheduled with your daughter..."

"Cancel the call with Beth," I tell him, feeling a slight twinge of guilt.

"You cancelled last week. And the week before..." Joel reminds me.

"Are you my Jiminy Cricket?" I ask, and only get silence. He has no idea what I'm talking about. Of course he doesn't. He's thirty years old.

"Look, it's not your job to remind me of my moral failings as a mother."

"I would never…" Joel sounds aghast. I'm hard on him, but I pay him well. I mentally add another hundred to his quarterly bonus. He's a good secretary and I want him to stay happy. He doesn't even complain about having to work weekends. As long as you pay people what they're worth, they usually stay content.

"Tell her I'm sorry and put another thousand in her account. Tell her to take her friends out to dinner or buy one of those new video game consoles for her dorm, or I don't know." I honk the horn at the slow car in front of me. "Whatever she wants. Tell her I will call her next week, come hell or high water."

Actually I shouldn't be so loose with that phrase, since both hell *and* high water hit us all over a decade ago. That and the onslaught of paranormal creatures. Some people saw it as the end of the world, while others welcomed the new frontier to explore. Especially sexually. Every woman who'd ever dreamed of having her very own Edward suddenly had a chance to bite into the forbidden apple. The divorce dockets filled up fast; we were doing Zoom divorces on our lunch breaks.

"Yes, ma'am. You'll call Beth next week," Joel says.

"Any messages from my husband?" I ask hopefully.

"Nothing since Friday. He checked into his hotel and said he'd be busy at the conference all weekend. Those big conference halls have terrible reception."

We're an independent family, always have been. No need to be in each other's business or spend every waking moment together. We each have our own lives and that's the way it's been for fifteen years. I have never been one to use the tracking apps that get so many spouses in trouble. Was never tempted…mostly because I knew my husband never would be, either. One of the things I love about Robert is that he's just as dedicated to his career as I am. While I work over eighty hours a week in the office, Robert is often gone on business trips. Meanwhile, we send our daughter to the best boarding school in New England. Maybe it's not exactly conventional, but I thought our life was perfect...until recently.

"I'll be out of reach for twenty minutes," I tell Joel.

"You're never out of reach," he says, shocked.

Of course he's suspicious. My phone is glued to my hand and my clients know that I can be called on at any time. Day or night. It's one of the reasons I have such a full client list, and a waiting period of six months before I can even do a sit-down with a new prospective client. I don't even have to advertise any more. I've got more referrals than I can handle and my word of mouth is off the charts. People hire me because they know the only difference between me and a pit bull...is the jewelry.

"Are you okay?" Joel asks. "It's not like you to—"

"I'm not dying, if that's what you mean. I don't have cancer and I'm not going in for a secret brain scan."

"I schedule all your doctor appointments, so I figured it wasn't health-related."

"I'm also not visiting a supernatural brothel."

"Good lord, of course not," Joel says, sounding sickened by the very idea, which I don't entirely appreciate. I mean, I do have a vagina.

"I'm available to everyone, all the time," I say, with a little more salt than necessary. "I don't think twenty minutes is too much to ask." I stop, take a breath. "Only call if it is an absolute emergency," I tell him. "If a client's case is about to crash and burn kind of emergency. Understand?"

"You got it, boss," Joel tells me.

I hang up and pull into the crappy strip mall and double check the address. This place? Really? There are cheap blinds in the windows, half of them bent. I can see a smear underneath the business logo on the window, roughly the height of either a grimy-fingered toddler or a very tall dog. Either way, having your child or your pet at your place of business does not bode well for the professional characteristics of this place. But my colleague swore they were the best.

I park and get out, looking around. I drive a nice car, a BMW, and I really hope no one breaks in while I'm here. Or tries to steal my rims, or whatever they do in bad neighborhoods. I clutch my purse close. I keep mace in the outer pocket. Anyone trying to mess with me will get a painful surprise. I'd even add a knee to the nuts if my pencil skirt would let my leg get that high.

I sigh; there was a time when this skirt used to bring my husband to his knees...and his face between mine. We especially enjoyed engaging in some slightly vanilla roleplay. For me, he'd be an Indiana Jones-type treasure hunter...not that far off from his hobby of hunting for exotic antiques. Robert, though, preferred to play dirty Judge. He'd confess to all sorts of crimes and then pleasure me in exchange for a lenient sentence. Of course, a lawyer isn't the same thing as a judge. Sometimes I wonder if the times that Robert and I enjoyed the most were the ones when we were pretending to be someone else.

I can't think about that right now, and I can't bring myself to go inside this dirty-windowed office just yet. If my two o'clock is pushed back to four that means I have an extra hour. I never have an extra hour. I should actually eat lunch.

I check my phone and there's a donut place around the

corner so I walk, keeping my chin up and a "Don't you dare mess with me" expression on my face the whole way there.

Yelp tells me the place has four full stars, and I quickly understand why. The sugary carby goodness is fantastic, like deep fried works of art. I toss a quick text to Joel, telling him to add a few dozen to next week's breakfast meeting. The staff will think they've died and gone to heaven...and hopefully hate me a bit less for all the overtime.

However, after I polish off not one, not two, but three donuts and about a gallon of mediocre coffee, I'm left with a stomachache.

I probably should've used the time to call my daughter instead of blasting through my calories for the day. But it's not just a lack of time that's kept me from logging in for our weekly chats.

Beth has always been oddly perceptive. My husband refers to her as our little witch. She's always had an ability—even as a little girl—to see right through the bullshit. Like when I got her a puppy when she was five. It was the most adorable basset hound in the world, from the top breeder in the country. Of course, I gave Beth the usual lecture about dogs being work and how we'd all have to take care of him.

She just petted his head and then looked at me and said in her little girl voice, "But Mommy, Margareta will take care of him, of course, just like she takes care of everything in the house." Before I could summon a response to this, she added in a thoughtful voice, "He will nicely balance out the family Christmas card photo. Father, Mother, child, and dog. One perfect happy family."

The words sent chills down my back, because they might have been stolen directly out of my head.

As she's gotten older, Beth hasn't lost any of her ability to see right through me. I hate to say that my own daughter makes me uncomfortable, but I could probably convince a jury that Beth is an actual witch—a supe—if I needed to, and it wouldn't just be my amazing skills at work.

Not that I would ever out my daughter. I love her.

But at the same time, I don't need her sniffing out my thoughts over the internet. I may not be mother of the year, but at least I can try and protect her from my suspicions. I walk back to my car and stare at the office window. The ill feeling in my stomach doesn't get any better and I vomit into the metal trash can on the sidewalk. I look like a drunk, maybe a donut drunk.

So embarrassing.

I sit in my car to regroup. I always have wipes and mouth-wash in the car. You can't show up to a deposition with coffee breath, and if I return to the office smelling like vomit and donuts, it's going to send Joel on some weird tangent where he thinks I have an eating disorder and sends me YouTube videos about managing my urges in a healthy way. A few weeks back, he "accidentally" sent me a clip about driving safety after I made it from the courthouse to the office in two minutes.

Crazy that this single thirty-year-old man is somehow better at parenting than I am.

It takes me a while to calm down and clean myself up. But time is precious and I need to put on my big girl panties and just get this over with. Although I kind of feel like all my panties have been of the sensible type lately. Mostly because I've been dressing for comfort rather than company—it's been a good long time since Robert has wanted to delve into my legal briefs.

With that thought, I take a deep breath and get out of the car, slamming the door determinedly.

I've never before seen a private investigator's office

paired with a cleaning service, but Eye Wide Open Investigations is the business my colleague recommended, so I put my doubts on hold, and head inside.

The interior isn't exactly what I would call reassuring. A woman in cut-off jean shorts that are about five inches too short for good taste is sitting on the lap of a man with an eyepatch who's seated at one of the desks. There's a woman at another desk, mostly hidden by several computer monitors and wearing a pair of clunky headphones that must be noise-cancelling. She seems totally oblivious to the man and woman who are engaged in some very inappropriate office behavior.

To my eyes this sort of lack of professionalism is a lawsuit waiting to happen. It's actually what I specialize in, going after the men—and very occasionally women—who don't understand that hitting on your work colleagues is a big no-no. But I'm not here today as the lawyer famous for bringing down the ass-grabbing predators of the business world.

"Excuse me," I say, my voice crisp as a Dalmanther comes around the side of the desk, his ears perked forward. "Jesus Christ on speakerphone," I shout, and jump onto a chair.

Dalmanthers are one of the side effects of supes living side by side with humans...and their pets. Except in this case, it was more like on top of each other. The rumor is that a panther shifter got too friendly with a Dalmatian and now the world has been gifted with Dalmanthers—extreme predators with the grace and hunting skill of a cat, but the loyalty and appearance of a dog.

I've handled more than a few cases of Dalmanthers gone bad—and some of them were very bad, indeed. Dalmanthers will protect their owners to the death, and sometimes maim people who just look at them funny.

The woman with the headphones gives me an annoyed look as I swing my purse at the Dalmanther. The couple behind the desk don't seem to notice anything more than each other just yet.

"Control your animal!" I say tightly, and the woman with the headphones shoves the right one aside.

"Shit, sit," she says, and the Dalmanther immediately does, but his eyes are on the brunette...who is on her boyfriend. Or husband. Or whatever they are.

This would not fly at my office. Absolutely nothing going on here is above board and I make yet another mental note to thank Joel for his professionalism when I get back. My eyes go to the Dalmanther—*if* I get back.

"I'm here to see..." I glance at the canoodling couple again. "The private investigator."

"Do I look like his secretary?" the woman with the headphones asks.

"You do," I tell her, arms crossed. How on earth did my colleague think that I would want to hire the services of a P.I. from such a place?

"I'm just I.T.," she tells me, then turns her head. "Yo, Paige. Nico," she shouts. "Customer." She promptly puts her headphones back on and returns to ignoring me.

Booty shorts woman, who must be Paige, turns toward me with an apologetic smile on her face. "Sorry," she says, her face red where the man's stubble had rubbed her. Then, patting the man on his cheek, she adds to him, "Lunch break is over, Nico."

She climbs off his lap and sashays back to the empty desk while he watches the sway of her backend until she's once again seated. Only then does he turn his attention to me, "Are you here for Supernatural Cleaning Services or a P.I.?" he asks.

"An investigator," I reply. And then for the first time, I say aloud the words that have been running inside my head for too long. "I think my husband is cheating on me."

3

Crystal

I'm a forty-year-old woman. I'm not afraid to tell my mother I got married.

Except I am just a little bit.

It's not that she's hard on me. The total opposite is true. Really the only time that Harmony—that's my mother's name—even raised her voice to me is when I tried to call her Mom. She doesn't believe in using general titles as names, and even preferred my tongue-tied attempts at Harmony when I was a toddler. I ended up calling her Nee until I was five.

Harmony loves me with all the power of creation and wants the very best for me. And I love her too. She taught me what it means to be a woman in this world, and how I have to stand on my own two feet and not have a man to lean on, because they can tip like that tower in Italy.

I hate disappointing her. And I think that me getting hitched would do just that. She's never let a man take her power, never tied herself down. I hate when she says, "Oh Crystal, my darling, what wicked forces have led you astray?" which seems to happen every time I start to consider getting serious with someone.

Especially since this time, she wouldn't have to ask; she'd know exactly what wicked force led me astray. She'd even know his name. Bobby—the man who swept me off my feet and convinced me to marry him. He's been at the house often enough. And she seems to like him just fine. But that was before we decided to do the big M. Harmony has always been perfectly okay with me doing the D. If I was more into the V, she'd support that as well.

But the M is a no-no.

Bobby and I eloped to Las Vegas. It was supposed to be my big birthday celebration, and he was looking for a way to make me feel better about turning the dreaded four oh.

But I wasn't really dreading it. I mean, why fear the passage of time?

Like I told Bobby, if I'm not getting older, that means I'm dead. Unless I'm a vampire, but I promised Harmony a long time ago I wouldn't fall for one of those forever young schemes. Turns out a lot of the guys selling immortality on the streets were just humans with fake teeth implants, and a lot of them claimed the path to the fountain of eternal youth was through their pants.

But I've never fallen for anything like that. The only thing I've ever done a deep dive on is Bobby. This amazing new man that swept into my life, promised me that forty was just the beginning of something wonderful, promised me a party, and then paid for the whole thing. First class flights and a lavish hotel room.

I'd never been to Vegas before and I was afraid it would

have bad juju, what with all those people drinking and gambling away their money. I thought it would reek of desperation, greed, and lust. But it's not that bad, or we came on a good weekend, because all I felt was happiness and hope.

You know when you're about to bite into a delicious piece of chocolate cake and the moment before you hit your lips is almost better than the taste itself? The anticipation. Vegas struck me with that feeling. You can practically taste it in the air. People were hopeful, at least. And that was more than I could say for the environment back home in New Jersey.

So we were drinking and gambling and having a hell of a time, when we passed one of those little chapels. Bobby got down on one knee right then and there and told me that he wanted me to be his wife. As much as my mother hates the institution of marriage, she always told me to follow my heart. So I did.

I followed my heart right into that chapel and into the arms of the man I love. I warned him that we'd have to break it slowly to Harmony, and he agreed. We wouldn't move in together yet and he'd let me tell her in the manner I saw fit.

He didn't push back on a single thing. In fact, he was absolutely elated at the boundaries that I set up. How did I find such an accommodating man?!

Well, it's not like my mother hasn't had her share of ill-fated love affairs. Not that mine will be ill-fated. But Harmony goes through men like they're tissues. Even though she's pushing sixty, she always has a string of lovers crawling over each other to get to her. I asked her once who my father was and she told me she is my mother and it really doesn't matter who the sperm donor was.

And while that might be the least romantic thing I've ever heard, I'd always vowed that my life would have love in it. Real love. The kind with a happily ever after and a kiss at the end. I didn't expect that kiss to be in front of an altar in Las Vegas with Elvis officiating, but whatever. I'm flexible, and that seems to be something that Bobby loves about me.

So yeah, Bobby and I had a weekend of fun and games. I wanted it to never end, and I even thought it might be fate when our flight was delayed a couple of hours. But Bobby seemed a bit put out. We sat at the airport bar while he swigged down half a bottle of vodka. Men are like that, if things don't go their way. I put five dollars in one of the slots and won fifty, so I knew I was on the right track. Life will let you know like that.

I always look for little indicators from the world around me, clues that let me know if the path I'm on is the right one or not. Clearly the universe was stepping in with that delayed flight, because fate doesn't just give you fifty dollars for no reason. But Bobby didn't share my enthusiasm for our extra hours together; his fingers drummed on his kneecaps through the entire flight, and he kept checking his phone, even though it was supposed to have been powered down.

But when we land he practically runs out of the gate, heading for baggage claim like it's a donut and cake buffet rather than the place where you lose your stuff and no one seems too worried about getting it back to you.

"I didn't expect the delay," he says, practically hopping up and down as we wait for the carousel to power on. "I scheduled a meeting."

"On a Sunday?" I ask.

He looks at me with that roguish smile. "Gotta pay for this trip somehow."

"I didn't need all that," I tell him. "I was going to celebrate my fortieth with a bottle of wine and some magic mushrooms Harmony has for communing with nature. You insisted on taking me to Vegas. Making it a big thing." I use a gentle voice to explain all this because getting angry will mess up my energy and Harmony will have to spend the whole afternoon cleansing my aura with her smudge sticks.

"I know you don't need anything from me," Bobby tells me. "And that's why I want to give you the moon." With a roguish grin, he adds, "And maybe a chance for us to sample some of those mushrooms together beneath it."

And just like that I melt into his arms. I don't care that we're in the middle of baggage claim, or who is looking. We kiss like it's the first time and when we pull apart I feel all wobbly.

"You work too hard," I tell him. "There's more important things in life."

"You've shown me that," he tells me. He pulls out some cash and gives it to me. "Do you mind catching a cab home?"

I don't...not really. But it feels like after the weekend we just spent in Vegas that this is a rather harsh return to reality.

Of course, Bobby is so sensitive to my needs, he immediately sees that I'm hurt and draws me into his arms and kisses me senseless once more. "I love you, you know that, don't you?" he tells me.

"And I love you," I tell him along with some other things too, about us being soul mates throughout time and history, reincarnated again and again. He gives me one of those smiles that means he doesn't believe in all that, but he loves that I do.

I deflate a bit on the ride home. It's hard not to when the

cab smells like someone might have either died or given birth in the backseat moments before. Harmony will be waiting for me. I've got to tell her that I'm now a Mrs., though of course I'm keeping my name. Crystal Thorne sounds ridiculous. Crystal Sky is the name Harmony gave me and that's the one I'll go to my grave with. I don't know how this works, though...am I Mrs. Crystal Sky? Or Crystal Sky "Mrs." Thorne? Can I use Mrs. like a street name? That might be kind of cool.

I open the door and smell the ginger biscuits. Harmony has tea ready for me. She always knows when I'm about to come home from a journey, whether I send her my flight itinerary or not.

I go to the sitting room, which is more like a greenhouse, and sit on a pillow across the coffee table from her. She pours me some tea.

"How was the cesspool?"

"It was good, not terrible at all. I didn't feel any bad juju. Not like you warned," I tell her.

She tilts her head at me. "A woman in love can overlook a lot of terrible things." I roll my eyes and sip my tea. When I'm done she grabs my cup and reads my tea leaves. She looks at me, her eyes boring into my soul.

"You gave your heart to the wrong man."

"Don't say that!" When I was only a little girl, she saw that my true love wouldn't come until I was in my fourth decade and he would be a love for the ages, soul mates, reincarnation, etc.

I met Bobby at the farmer's market four months ago. I was working my mother's booth, Harmony Crystals and Palm Readings. We always sell a lot there, especially to women who actually want to use the healing powers, but a lot of them just want something pretty to put in their house.

But we usually don't get handsome, well-dressed men eager to peruse our offerings.

I knew, as soon as I saw him, that Bobby was the one who'd been foretold.

First off, he bought my two favorite crystals. Amethyst which is used for calming and cleansing the spirit. And the second, bloodstone, which sounds bad but is used to energize and align your soul. Used together, they make you feel like you've been reborn.

Secondly, he confessed that he was just a week into his vegan journey. I always knew I could never be with a meat eater and the fact that he made this change right before our meeting, was clearly fate sending out a signal.

But the thing that sealed the deal was when he asked me out, before saying yes, I asked to see his palm. This is something Harmony taught me. Everything you need to know about a man is printed on the palm of his hand—or so she says.

I focused on his love line and my heart broke when I saw the way it branched off in every direction. This was a man with a traveling heart. I told him what I saw and he got real sad and quiet. The twinkle that had been in his eyes faded right out of existence. Just like that, I was ready to cry too. Strong emotions always affect me that way.

Anyway, he said he was sorry for bothering me and that I was right—he wasn't good enough for me. He'd been married two other times and was a loser in love both times.

I saw then that he might be a heartbreaker, but he'd had his heart broken too.

I told him I'd go out with him.

And now...only a few months later—we're married.

"I have to tell you something," I say. And before I can lose my nerve I let it out. "Bobby and I got married."

I thought she might be disappointed, or even be a little angry, which I almost never see her get. But her pitying look is so much worse.

"You've chosen a hard path, daughter. By midnight, you'll be a widow."

4

———

Maddie

My feet hurt, and half the people have left the party, but Bert still hasn't shown up.

He's always late, known for it so much that hardly anyone batted an eye when he wasn't at his own vow renewal. But I'm starting to get a little worried.

Growing up, he was the boy next door. Two years older and a million years more cool and sophisticated. Even as a three-year-old I worshipped him. At twelve I knew he was out of my league. But still, I couldn't stop myself from wanting him. And then in high school, amazingly, he broke his leg skiing and while he was laid up at home, we became close friends and then more than friends.

We took a break when he went off to college. But when he was home for the summer after freshman and then sophomore year, we'd start up again.

And then I got knocked up. Instead of starting college with Bert, I started Lamaze classes. And we got married, of course. Because my parents weren't going to have it any other way. Bert hadn't even batted an eye when they suggested that he make an honest woman out of me. Instead, he smiled and told them that was the plan all along —marrying me had always been the end goal. Charmed, they believed him. And so did I. Then I had Nathan, and a few years later, the twins, Daniel and Catrina—Carrie for short. And not that long ago, though he's in high school now, Oliver.

Not even thirty and my whole life seemed settled.

I was looking forward to the suburban dream when the world fell apart and supes showed up. A lot of families struggled, and there were some really tough times. Not only were there natural disasters and violence between the new species, but the economy tanked, and a lot of families in our neighborhood couldn't keep up with their house payments anymore.

Bert was one of the lucky ones. He didn't just survive, he thrived. His antiques shop became a magical items shop. He procured all kinds of supernatural things for all kinds of people. He'd deal with anyone, supes and humans alike— and he was rewarded for it. We thrived.

We got a bigger house and a bigger storefront. The antiques shop became the antiquities shop. The kids were sent to better schools, and then on to great colleges. With only Ollie at home, and him almost an adult, I started working at the shop. Bert traveled more and more, going all over the world looking for treasures to fill it with. Amazingly, I fell in love with the work. I even convinced Bert to let me open a shop next door for vintage clothing, which I argued was a different sort of treasure.

All in all, life is good. The kids are raised into good people. The business is thriving. And Bert...well I love him as much as I ever did. A lot of people ask how we can still so clearly be in love after twenty-five years together. Maybe it's distance that keeps the heart so fond. He's out of town more often than he's in it, so anytime we can spend together is precious.

It also helps that he's a hopeless romantic. He makes a big deal out of birthdays and anniversaries, going all out to make them special.

Which brings us back to today. It's not the first time that Bert planned a big party for me only to be a no-show. My fortieth birthday a few years back had a circus theme, complete with a trapeze act set up in the backyard. He was supposed to fly in that afternoon, but his flight got delayed. I wasn't angry—Maddie doesn't get mad—but I was disappointed. And he knew it. That's when he came up with the vow renewal. There was no way he could or would miss it.

Except he did.

For six months I dieted to try and fit back into my original wedding dress. It didn't happen because my eighteen-year-old body was of a shape so different from my post-childbirth forty-three-year-old body. I'd have to get bones removed to fit in that dress again. I did however, find a vintage flowy white dress with embroidered flowers all across the bodice. It's lovely. The type of thing my mother would've called hippy-dippy, but I don't care. Paired with a pretty lily flower crown with a short veil attached, I felt beautiful. Like a forest sprite.

Now though, I just feel stupid. A foolish middle-aged woman standing in the middle of a forest in kitten heels sunk deep into muck, getting eaten alive by mosquitos, and dodging pixies who are looking hungry in a different way. They sometimes will touch a person and take a little of their vitality and youth. Or "beauty," as they call it. The pixie gets high and the person feels like they're coming down with the flu.

I glare in the direction of the pixies, daring them to come near me...while also feeling a bit hurt that they haven't tried. Don't I look like I have enough beauty to give them a decent buzz?

"I'm sorry...about Dad," Carrie says, interrupting my increasingly dark thoughts. "Do you want me to stay and help clean up?"

"No, go. I know you want to hang out with your boyfriend."

"Mom." Carrie rolls her eyes. "We're not official yet."

"Uh-huh," I answer.

But I know that look. I know how her voice gets higher when she talks about him. Carrie and Britney were best friends, but when Britney came out as trans and changed to Brandon...well. Something changed in their relationship. A mother knows.

Brandon had family stuff today so couldn't come to the ceremony, but that was hours ago. "Go see if he's free now," I tell her. She gives me a big hug.

"Why don't you ever get mad at Dad?" she asks. "I'm pissed at him right now."

"What your father and I have works," I tell her, once again pushing down all the hurt and anger, explaining away why Bert has once again let us down. I'm fairly certain it won't be the last time, either.

I feel a warmth in my chest, something I remember from childhood...I'm pretty sure it's anger. I take a deep breath, shove it back down. I didn't win Bert Thorne by being angry at him, and I'm not the kind of woman who any man would ever refer to as "the ball and chain," or his "old lady." I'm kind, caring, and forgiving—yes, maybe to a fault—but I claimed the prize of Bert Thorne by taking care of him when we were teenagers, and if I've been doing it ever since then—

Well...maybe it is my own fault.

I take a look at the rows of empty chairs, the little lilies so carefully painted onto the backrests. I want to lift one up and throw it around, bang it against a tree and then stomp on the pieces. But even with everyone gone and no one to witness my tantrum, the very logical side of me knows that while it might feel good, after I've thrown my fit, I'm the one who will be left to pick up the very literal pieces—plus a fine from the church for obliterating a chair.

With everyone gone I turn off the fairy lights and pull one of the chairs out to the middle of the clearing. A last, slightly punch-drunk pixie buzzes past me, her loop-de-loops growing more exaggerated as she spins lazily in the air.

I look up at the stars. The moon is full, with an eerie red tinge. A blood moon.

A shiver runs through me and I realize the temp has dropped. I should get moving, warm up. But I can't face all the clean-up work. Not alone. Something pricks at my eyeballs and I'm reminded of another feeling from child-hood—sadness. I haven't cried over a man since the first time Bert kissed me, because he promised I would always be happy.

And I am...right?

My phone beeps and I grab it from the hidden pocket I'd sewn in the dress. Must have gotten a bit of reception finally. I know it's Bert. I know what he'll say. And I know I'll forgive him.

It's a message from him, but it's not the apology I'm expecting.

I've been taken by some bad people. They want one of the artifacts. Go to the shop and get the bronze globe from the safe. Bring it to me at eleven pm sharp. My life depends on it. I'll text you where.

I sit up, the chilly night air blowing through my body and freezing my soul.

I'm going to be able to save the day, sweep in and take care of Bert the way I did twenty-five years ago when he was laid up with that broken leg. I still remember the expression on his young, unlined face when he told me, "I don't know what I'd do without you, Maddie."

He'd needed me then. And for the first time in my life I'd felt not like the forgettable middle child, but instead as if I was someone necessary and irreplaceable. Like only I had the power to soothe Bert's pain and that he literally could not survive without me.

Nathan was conceived that night. Maybe I've been waiting since then for Bert to need me like that again. Maybe this is our true vow renewal ceremony.

I stand, feeling invigorated, a chorus of "my man needs me" running through my head.

Don't worry baby. Here I come.

5

———

Helena

As soon as I declared that I was a woman in need of a P.I. to catch a cheating husband, Paige—she of the shorty shorts—shoots me a look that could boil water in Russia.

"Nico doesn't offer those services anymore," she tells me, her eyes narrowing.

"What services? I thought you were a private investigator. Surely it's not good business for a P.I. to turn away adultery cases?" I must look adequately perplexed and miserable because her face softens and her tone changes.

"You're not here for the ex-wife special? The secret menu order with sexy sauce? The werewolf ride? The private dick's dick?" she asks, going through this extraordinary list as she ticks the items of one hand.

Maybe it's the lawyer in me, but I like to have all the facts. And I do not like being interrogated. Pulling myself up tall, with my back ramrod straight, and my expression in full bitch mode, I stare at Paige like she's an unruly witness.

"Are you suggesting that this man—" I point to Nico—an admittedly handsome one with the eye patch. "Is he some sort of private investigator prostitute? He's actually a gigolo?"

"No, I am not a gigolo," Nico says, standing up behind his desk.

"You kinda were," Paige shoots back at him.

With a low growl he stalks toward Paige and I realize that her mention of werewolf ride was not a euphemism. This man is definitely a shifter and right now he looks like a dangerous animal intent on his prey. Paige, though, doesn't give an inch. In fact, when Nico comes to a stop directly in front of her, she actually has the temerity to boop his nose. In response Nico growls again and then with a speed that only a supe could be capable of, he sweeps her into his arms.

"Maybe you shouldn't have waited so long to claim me," he says to her in a low voice.

Winding her arms around his neck, Paige smiles. "The other day you said the anticipation was part of the fun. The thrill of the hunt and all that." She flutters her eyelashes at him in an exaggerated fashion, flirting with him. They just enjoy being together. Being in love, which they so very clearly are. In the first flush of it, if I'm not mistaken.

I can't help but think of the heady early days of my relationship with Robert. Supes were just coming out of hiding and the whole world felt like it was on the verge of collapse. Up till then I'd been a single-minded career woman. Sure, I liked men and enjoyed their company, but I hadn't yet met one that was worth the trouble of keeping him around permanently.

Then I met Robert at a supes and human business mixer, geared toward forward thinkers who realized the world had changed and instead of seeing it as a threat, recognized it as an opportunity.

He wasn't intimidated by my confidence and focus. In fact, it's what he liked most about me because he was the same way, focused on starting up his own business procuring and selling antiques.

And I liked that he didn't use some cheesy pickup line. Instead, the first thing he said to me was, "I overheard you discussing with that ogress the legalities of running her own brothel. I hope that's not a breach of client-attorney privileges."

Okay, maybe it was a bit of a pickup line. But it wasn't cheesy. And when I explained to him that I was just offering advice even though that wasn't my area of specialty, he was quick to ask if I might give him some advice as well. We ended up talking all night. And into the next day. Then the one after that as well.

Of course, we did more than talk. We couldn't get enough of each other. Usually sex was like any other need. I ate when I was hungry. Slept when I was too tired to keep my eyes open any longer. And had sex when I was horny.

But Robert was an itch I couldn't stop scratching. What was that one cheesy line from that movie? He completed me.

I married him. Had a child with him. Side by side we grew our careers together. We were perfect partners in life and love.

Except somehow, at some point...the love seemed to fall away. We're no longer new and shiny. I don't count the days when he's gone. And I don't run into his arms when he returns. I don't miss my husband...and maybe that's what bothers me the most.

I'm an all-out, steel-willed bitch, but I was also in love,

and it was nice to have a part of my life that allowed me to be softer, warmer, and kinder.

I miss the *feeling* of missing him. Of being wildly crazily in love. And seeing Paige and Nico once again oblivious to the people around them, only feels like salt in the wound.

"I was thinking of running away, just so you could have the fun of chasing and catching me all over again," Paige says to him now.

"See how far you'll make it," he tells her, a challenge in his eyes.

"Actually," I interrupt. "Maybe you can wait until after I leave to finish playing grabass together."

They both look up at me and blink like they're coming out of a dream.

Finally, Paige points a finger at Nico. "It was your fault this time!"

He holds his hands up. "Guilty." Then with a grin, he adds, "Although when you wear those shorts—"

Before they can get going again, I step between them. "Hi. Woman who is afraid her husband is cheating on her, let me re-introduce myself. I have money and I'll pay extra if you two would stop making googly eyes at each other for just ten minutes."

"Impossible," comes the voice of the I.T. woman from behind the bank of computer screens. "Dogs in heat have more restraint."

The Dalmanther trots to Paige's side and barks, as if in agreement.

"Don't start," she tells him. "I can still have you fixed."

"Ignore Hepa," Paige adds and then indicates a chair in front of Nico's desk. "Please sit down. Can I get you something to drink? Water? Coffee? Beer?"

"Beer," I hear myself say, even though I'm more of a fine

white wine type of woman. But right now something cold and frosty and a bit more lowbrow seems to fit. My choice seems to make Paige like me more—either that or she's finally convinced I'm not here to steal her man. Not that anyone could; he clearly only has eyes—er, eye—for her. I glance at Nico's eyepatch, suddenly understanding the Eye Wide Open business name.

Nico meanwhile reaches into a small fridge, pulls out a bottle, and pops the cap with the tip of his thumb. After handing it to me, he takes a seat behind his desk while Paige perches on the edge of it.

"Tell us about your husband," Nico says.

"We've been married sixteen years now. I thought we were happy, even if we don't exactly have a traditional marriage."

"Go on," Paige prompts.

"I met Robert when I was thirty. I was working eighty-hour weeks, on the fast track for a partnership. I didn't have time for romance or a family, but Robert swept me off my feet. He didn't care that I could only see him once a week."

"But you think he got tired of that?" Nico asks. "At some point it stopped being enough?"

I nod. "Even when I had Elizabeth—that's our daughter—he was a fantastic stay-at home-dad. We had a nanny, sure, so he could have some time to himself, but he was the primary caregiver. It worked for us. Now with Beth in boarding school, I think he's let himself...wander."

"Specifics will help," Nico tells me.

"What exactly makes you think that he's cheating?" Paige asks, kindly. "I know it's not easy. But if you could give us some more concrete information that would help."

I sigh. There's no smoking gun. No lipstick on his collar.

"It's just a feeling," I admit. "But in my job, I've learned to trust my gut."

Paige nods. "Sometimes that's all it takes." She glances at Nico.

"A fishing expedition like this isn't cheap," Nico warns.

I let out a little hysterical laugh. I haven't worried about money since I paid off my student loans. For ten years, before I met Robert, I didn't spend money on anything except my little studio apartment and the suits I needed for work. Even after we got married and Beth came along, with all the vacations and school fees and trips for Robert I have a nice little nest egg squirrelled away.

"I can pay," I assure him.

"No, I mean, do you really want to shell out a bunch of money to find out that your feeling is wrong?"

Secretly, I thank him for not vocalizing the opposite— that I might also pay a lot of money to find out I'm right.

"What about finding out that your feeling was wrong, but also right?" Paige asks.

I frown. "Clarify."

"Well maybe he's not cheating, but he's in a secret vampire cult," she says.

Nico nods. "That was our last case. She thought he had cancer, because of his low energy, but it turned out it was vampires sucking him dry."

"He got off on it," Paige adds. "So it was sort of a form of cheating. Would it be upsetting to you if it wasn't physical cheating, but some form of an emotional affair?"

"Of course it would be upsetting," I tell them. "But I can take it. Whatever he's up to, no matter how bad it is. I want to know."

"Alright, let's get started..." He pulls out a notebook while Paige wanders over to her desk, the Dalmanther sitting patiently at her feet. I realize that she must be the other half of this business—Down & Dirty Supernatural Cleaning Services. I can't imagine scrubbing a floor on your hands and knees in shorts like that, but whatever. It's clearly working for her. I steal a glance at Nico. And working quite well.

Forty-five minutes later I've told Nico every minute detail of our lives. I also gave him a hefty deposit.

As I drive back to the office I can't help but laugh at myself. Nico had kindly warned me again that some wives learn things they didn't want to know. It must have been a slow day for Paige, because she wandered back into our area to tell me about the man who was paying an ogre to feed him baby food while he sat in her oversized booster seat, wearing a bib.

It was so ridiculous I laughed out loud, and it also made me realize that Robert would never do anything like that... or maybe even anything like I'm afraid of at all.

Me and my feeling. What was I thinking?

I could turn around and call the whole thing off. I could even just call and tell them to rip up the check.

But I don't.

If it puts my mind at ease, then I guess it's worth the price. And hopefully, someday soon, I can laugh over my silly, unfounded fears.

The rest of the day flies by. I have my clients and I make sure to tell Joel that his overtime is not overlooked, that he'll be fairly compensated. My secretaries burn out fast; they can't take the hours and the stress, but I try to make them as comfortable as I can while they're with me. I also refuse to let Joel stay as late as I do. I can get by on five hours of sleep, but Joel needs a solid eight at least. I send him home a little after eight and tell him to enjoy his evening.

I'm the only one in the office when my phone vibrates.

It's Robert. *I need you.* We sext sometimes to keep the romance alive when I'm working long hours. Although, I have to admit, it's been a while.

Picking up my phone, my fingers fly across the screen. *Show me.*

I start to flick open the buttons on my blouse, so I can have a pic ready for him too. But his next text isn't the close-up of his dick that I was expecting.

Instead he writes *You know that paperweight I gave you for your office? I need you to bring it to me.* That is not at all what I was expecting.

I look at the thing. It's an ugly sun symbol made out of gold. Robert likes to go antiquing in his free time, and when he found this thing he said he thought it would suit my office. I hated it, but I didn't tell him that. Instead I dutifully put it on my desk next to the picture of us posing with Beth on one of her birthdays.

I pick it up. It's clunky and heavy and it's always kind of creeped me out, to be honest.

Why? I text. *I'm working. It will have to wait.*

I see the ellipsis that means he's typing.

I wouldn't ask if it wasn't important. I need it or it's the end of me.

I'm even more confused by this. Is he teasing me? Is he trying to relight the old Indiana Jones role play?

It's a matter of life and death.

I call him but he doesn't answer. Staring at the bulky sun thing I call him again and again.

Finally he answers. His voice is tight.

"Helena, please, listen. I need you to bring it at midnight. On the dot. Not early. Not late. Not—" I'm about to jump in to tell Robert I understand what "on the dot" means without him breaking it down for me. But before I can, Robert goes silent and a new voice comes on.

"Bring me the zodiac sun or your husband will die. We will tell you where shortly."

The line goes dead.

I sit in stunned silence. How could I have been so stupid? Robert isn't cheating on me, he's wrapped up in something much much worse.

Regret is quickly replaced with determination. No way am I just going to sit by the phone like some scared little woman. Already, my brain is whirring, coming up with plans.

Because I'm not going to just save Robert—I'm going to make the people who took him regret that they ever messed with my man.

6

———————

Crystal

The front door opens and one of my mother's regular clients comes down the front steps. Mrs. Manning has been paying for readings for at least twenty years. She says that before she found us, she tried therapy, yoga, and recreational drugs. But none of it steered her in the right direction or brought her the happiness that came when Harmony Sky's star readings did.

"Crystal, you look like you're absolutely glowing!" Mrs. Manning tells me. "What have you been up to?"

"No good," my mother mumbles.

I roll my eyes. "I got married this weekend."

Mrs. Manning *squees* and congratulates me and searches my finger for a ring. But I agree with Harmony, a ring is a chain that society places on women to show that they belong to someone. No way was I getting a ring.

"What do you think of a husband who doesn't want to live with his wife?" Harmony asks.

"That *is* strange," Mrs. Manning agrees.

"What do you think of a mother who would rather have her daughter be a widow than a wife?"

Mrs. Manning looks between us; she clearly doesn't want to take sides and risk annoying Harmony. "I'm sure your mother has her reasons for—"

"Nope!" I interrupt, which is rude and not like me, but Harmony always taught me that speaking one's inner truth is more important than good manners. "She didn't scry it or see it in the stars—it was my tea leaves, and those can be kind of unreliable."

"Hmm..." Mrs. Manning says. "Your mother is very perceptive..."

"Yes," I agree, but then quickly add—more for Harmony's benefit than for Mrs. Manning, "But she always says that she must never speak for the universe, but rather let it speak through her."

"Those seem like the same thing?" Poor Mrs. Manning looks confused.

Harmony points to the door. "Crystal, your energy is becoming ugly. Please leave the room and close the door behind you."

Head held high, I do as she asks. Honestly, I feel a little bit bad for getting in the way of Mrs. Manning's reading. But I had to say something. I'd retreated to the bathroom—the only room with a lock—after Harmony dropped that bomb about my becoming a widow. It was such an awful thing to hear. But then after thinking about it, I marched back out and demanded to see the tea leaves for myself. That's when Harmony admitted that she hadn't exactly seen this precise prediction in my leaves. Rather she saw the symbol for 12 and then sort of embroidered the rest of the message about Bobby dying.

I hate to think this of my own mother, but I think it was

more of a wish than a prediction. It would be really upsetting if I thought it was because she wishes Bobby himself ill. But I know it's just the institution of marriage.

Still, I had to draw a line and let her know that kind of talk is not okay with me. Bobby is my husband and he's not going anywhere. She needs to get used to that fact.

Upstairs in my room, I open my suitcase and inhale the scent of Vegas. I never thought the smell of stale cigarette smoke could make me feel nostalgic. I don't have a lot to unpack, I like to travel light, but I hoist my suitcase onto my bed and take out the one thing that Bobby gave me as a wedding gift.

It's a large hefty metal circle with a hole in the middle, about a foot across. I guess it is a ring of sorts. But on the metal is engraved all the zodiac signs. It has the symbol for each sign on the inner circle, then the constellation for the sign is on the outside. I love it.

It really is the perfect gift. And the fact that Bobby learned a little bit about his sign says it all. I'm a Cancer, which means that I'm extremely intuitive. Psychic almost. My ruling planet is the moon.

I almost didn't go for Bobby when I found out he was a Leo. Leos are ruled by the sun...so usually we're as different as night and day. But *opposites attract* is a saying for a reason. I explained to Bobby how we're like oil and water but he just said, that's how you make salad dressing, and left it at that.

And of course, who wants a salad without the dressing?

I hear a shout from the other room. I stop unpacking and run to find Mrs. Manning upset and my mother not even trying to calm her.

"Harmony! What is going on?"

"She told me not to go out tonight. She said something bad was gonna happen."

"To you?" I ask. Usually my mother's readings aren't that specific.

"I told her it was an ill-fated night from this blood moon," Harmony explains. "But she wants to go to some art exhibit. The only safe place to be tonight is in the protection of your home."

"But...I thought...tonight would be the night." Mrs. Manning is separated from her husband but she thinks that they are going to reconcile. Even I can see it's only a matter of time before they do. I feel a little bad because my mother is the one who put the notion in her head that her husband was cheating. And of course he was, but he dumped the other woman and promised to be true. Mrs. Manning was just waiting for the right chance to take him back.

"Look, why don't you change your plans? A nice home-cooked dinner? Just the two of you. Mr. Manning will jump at the opportunity."

She tilts her head. "Yes. I wanted to meet somewhere neutral, but if you really think I need to stay home..."

"I really do," Harmony tells her.

"Then I'll invite him over. It's time we got on with our lives."

Harmony gives me a grateful smile and walks Mrs. Manning to the door.

"What was that about?" I ask.

"Just a feeling," she tells me. "Tonight is not the night to go out. Stay home."

"I wasn't going anywhere," I assure her. "I just got back!"

The landline rings and I answer. My mother refuses to get a cell phone. "Harmony Crystals and Palm Reading."

"Crystal?" Bobby's voice asks breathlessly.

What a good husband, making sure I got back safely. I should tell him to head straight home tonight as soon as his meeting is over, or to come here. Most of the time my mother's readings are not something that should be ignored.

"Hey, babe," I answer.

Bobby's voice comes over strained and frantic. "Crystal, I need you to bring your wedding gift to me. It's important."

Bobby deals in artifacts and it's weird that he'd give me a present and then want it back, but it's possible he found out it was worth way more than he originally thought, and I'm not materialistic. He must have a good reason for asking; and he did pay for that entire trip.

"Okay, sure. Tomorrow?"

"No. Tonight."

"I'm bone tired," I say, uneasy. "And my mother warned me that there's an ill omen in the air. I'm not leaving the house tonight."

"You have to, babe. Some bad people have me and they want that artifact. If you don't bring it..." he trails off.

"What have you gotten mixed up in?" I ask, my heart picking up a beat. My mother's prediction echoes through my mind. *By midnight, you'll be a widow.* Suddenly, I'm not so sure that she made it all up.

"I'll explain later but you have to bring it to me tonight. Meet me at one a.m. I know you won't be early, but please, baby, don't be late."

"I understand," I say, a little hurt that he thinks I wouldn't be punctual for something this important. I mean, sure, time is a human construct and the more we try to control it, the more we simply tie ourselves into knots. But since Bobby seems to already be tied up, I can make an exception this time.

"I'll text you the address. Where's your cell phone?"

"Charging in the other room," I tell him.

"Keep it on you."

"I will. You know I'll do anything for you," I tell him.

"That's my girl. I love you, babe. One o'clock. Don't be late."

I hang up to find Harmony at my shoulder. "You are not going to meet him," she orders. For a moment I'm stunned silent. My mother giving any kind of command is shocking.

Finally I gather my wits. "I will and I am," I tell her.

"I knew that man would bring you down. I knew he was no good for you. But you didn't want to listen. You are not leaving this house tonight, young lady."

"You wait until I'm forty years old to act like a mother?" I shake my head. "My husband needs me and I'm going to him."

She knows I'm determined, so she relents and stomps off, only to return a few moments later with my grandmother's pearl necklace and earrings.

"Wear these," she demands.

Pearls are my lucky gems, and though I don't really like looking like a fifties housewife, I put them on to please her.

She puts her hand on my chin and looks into my eyes. "Crystal, promise me you will not put yourself in danger for an unworthy man."

"I promise," I lie. Because I know the truth.

I would die to protect Bobby Thorne.

7

———

Maddie

Crap on a cracker—my minivan won't start.

I try all the tricks that usually work.

I pump the gas pedal as I turn the ignition.

I put it into neutral and let it roll a few feet, as if to let the damn thing know that forward movement is what I'm aiming for.

I even pull out the witch charm I bought at a flea market a few months back in a moment of desperation. I read the incantation several times before trying once more to get the van to start.

This time the engine turns over, but then with a cough and shake—it dies once more.

Damn it.

Bert's been telling me to get a new vehicle for years now. And I've wanted to. It's not like I enjoy driving around a beaten-up minivan that spends more time in the shop than in my driveway. But every time I'm ready to pull the trigger, Bert beats me to it. A few years back he bought a BMW, which he insisted was a business expense. I explained to him that the IRS wouldn't see it that way. But, of course, I understood. Part of his business is projecting an air of success. I worked the new payments into our budget and was on track to pay it off early when...he traded it in for a Tesla.

A piece of me wanted to scream and tell him to take it right back to the dealership. But instead I agree with him that we had to do our part to protect the environment and the planet.

Now, though, that damn Tesla might end Bert's life. It's already ten o'clock. It will take me at least thirty minutes to get to the store. If I have to wait for someone to come out here and pick me up...

There's a knock at my window. I shriek and turn to see a large man looming outside. Slamming down the locks, I yell, "Get away! I have a gun!"

It's not true. But I need something to counter the truth—which is that I'm a woman alone in the middle of nowhere.

It must work because the man takes a step back and raises his hands up high. "Don't shoot, Darlin'," he says, his voice deep and smooth with a thick and syrupy Southern drawl. "I just came over to offer my help."

I blink as the moonlight reveals his beautiful face. Good lord, he's handsome. And I recognize him. He's the man who arrived late—my sister's date.

Cranking the window down a few inches—for once I'm happy for the outdated technology in my old van—I say to the man, "Is Stephy still here?"

"Stephy?" he repeats, looking confused.

"My sister?" I say, the feeling of danger rising once more. "Weren't you her date?"

He blinks and then smiles revealing a dimple. It's such a

discordant element on his otherwise chiseled and elegant face. I stare at it for a moment, mesmerized, and with an odd yearning to touch it.

"Yes, I was your sister's date. I'm sorry, I don't think of her as Stephy." He shudders. "I much prefer to use her full name. I understand from what she said that terrible nicknames are a family tradition. Your younger brother is Tick, right? And of course, everyone calls you—"

"Maddie," I say with him, as relief floods through my system. Cleary, if he knows all our names, he's not a stranger. Rolling the window down the rest of the way, I hold out a hand. "I'm sorry I didn't come by earlier to introduce myself. I'm usually a better hostess..."

He takes my hand in both of his and presses a kiss to the top of it. "You are not a Maddie," he tells me.

Pulling my hand back and knowing that I'm blushing like a teenager, I mumble, "I know, because I never get mad."

"Never, huh?" he laughs. "That explains the sense of danger surrounding you. All women are volcanoes, but you're a dormant one." Reaching through my window, he traces a finger along my collar bone. "Waiting to explode." He leans in closer and adds in a low intimate voice, "Your husband is a fool."

With a gasp I jerk away from his touch. My husband! Bert! He's kidnapped and waiting for me and I'm—

Flirting? Is that what this is?

I've always thought of flirting as something light—a chocolate mousse. But this is dark and heavy and dangerous. A molten chocolate lava cake of desire.

What is wrong with me!?

This man is at least a good ten years younger than me. He's dating my sister. And even if those two things weren't true—I'm happily married. Well...I'm married. As for the happily part—I'm working on that.

I shake these thoughts away and replace them with the practical ones that rule my life. They fit me as comfortably as an old pair of pants and yet for a moment I resent their return. Good, boring Maddie with two feet firmly on the ground. You can always count on her to come through.

Bert is counting on me, I remind myself.

"My van won't start," I tell this man—I realize he hasn't given me a name. "Could you give me a lift? I desperately need a ride to my shop."

He lifts an eyebrow. "On a Sunday evening?"

I shrug helplessly. "Monday comes fast. I like to be prepared." Something else occurs to me. "That is if Stephy doesn't mind...she's not waiting on you..."

"No, we parted ways amicably at the end of your lovely party."

"You broke up?" I ask, surprised and also a little bit relieved.

"It was never nothing that formal," he replies. "We never had that spark. You know the spark I'm talkin' about?" His hand lands on top of mine.

Good lord, this man is touchy feely and with every connection—

Stopping that thought, I start to crank up the window, putting a barrier between us. But it can't last. I'll have to travel in this man's car with him oozing sexuality the whole way. Not that I'd ever truly be tempted by him. Nor him by me. I'm sure he gives every woman he meets this treatment, gazing at her with his dark liquid eyes as if she is an object of infinite mystery and fascination.

Which I most definitely am not.

I am staid and middle-aged. I threw away all my sexy

bras and panties years ago, realizing that Bert didn't care about them. He's always been more of a wham, bam, thank you ma'am type of man. Even worse, I like it this way. Or at least, I don't dislike it. Bert owns my heart and my body came along with it by necessity. The sex part of our relationship has never felt essential to who we are.

I'm pretty sure the man in front of me would not understand that. I'm a minivan of a woman and he's a—

Crotch rocket.

This is what I see parked in the shadow of my van when I climb out, refusing his outstretched hand.

"A motorcycle?" I say, my dismay clear in my voice.

"I'm an expert ride," he assures me. "And you can have my helmet."

I gulp. "Please tell me you have a sidecar stashed in the bushes."

This earns a grin, once again showing off his dimple. "Sadly no. I've been told that such an addition would destroy my badass image."

Badass image, the words echo in my head. I cannot ride all the way back to town with this man. I cannot. "There's a gas station up the street. If you could take me that far, I'll be able to call one of my children—"

"Maddie—" He flinches as if my name causes him pain. "We must find another name for you."

I laugh, admittedly a bit hysterically. "Maybe we should figure out yours first?"

He joins me in laughter, though his is warm and thick like chocolate fudge. "Well day-umn, I was so wound up in your name, I forgot all about my own." He holds out a hand to me. "Let's try this again."

I take his hand in mine and give it a quick pump, making

it clear that this one is all business—no more kissing my knuckles. "Maddie."

"I'm Aden," he says, still holding my hand, though I'm trying to take it back. "And you are Madeline, but that doesn't fit you either." Finally he releases me and I am stupidly disappointed he didn't force the kiss.

Turning, he slings a leg over the bike and sits. "Come on." He pats the small bit of space left on the seat behind him.

Not seeing any alternative, I climb onto the back, much more awkwardly than he did, as I have to bunch the skirt of my wedding dress around my legs to keep from flashing my underwear. I try to keep some space between us, but it's impossible; the seat slides me forward until my front is pressed to his back.

"Um..." I say.

"You're gonna want to hold on tight," Aden tells me.

"To what?" I ask, feeling around my legs for some sort of hand bar or seatbelt.

He laughs and I can feel it in my belly. "To me," he says as the engine roars to life beneath me. "Put this on too," Aden adds, handing back the helmet. I shove it onto my head and then tentatively grip the back of his shirt.

"Okay," I yell to him. "I'm ready." I squeeze my eyes shut and remind myself that I'm doing this for Bert.

The motorcycle jerks forward and I nearly fly off—it's only Aden snaking a hand back to grab me that keeps me seated.

"I told ya to hold on tight!" he calls back. But he doesn't need to tell me twice. This time I don't hesitate to wrap my arms around him, hugging his middle like my life depends on it.

The forest on either side of us begins to fly by as we gain

speed. I want to tell him to slow down, but I'm already running behind. It would take a miracle and a time machine for me to get to Bert by his 11pm deadline.

I can only hope that his kidnappers are understanding about car trouble.

8

Helena

Thank goodness Joel isn't here when I walk out with the giant sun. When I put it in my office he'd grimaced and said, "Oh no, did another client try to pay you with some ugly old antique from their attic?"

The poor guy turned ten shades of red when I told him it was a gift from my husband.

I plunk the thing into the passenger seat, and one of the rays slices my finger.

"Ouch!" I leap back, sucking at the wound. My own blood is hot and metallic in my mouth, and there's plenty of it, but I don't even consider checking to see if I need stitches; there's no time.

I hop behind the wheel and shoot a quick text to Robert's number. I don't know who is on the receiving end, but they said they would let me know where to bring this thing—whatever it is. I pull a scarf out of my glovebox; luckily there are still some there from when Robert and I used to grab a quickie in the parking lot at lunch, and I'd need to cover stubble burns on my neck in order to go back to work. Now though, it's just catching my blood.

I spot an empty parking spot and pull off the road, waiting for further instructions, and check my finger.

I don't think I need stitches, but I should probably make sure my tetanus shot is up to date. Who knows where Robert got this thing. His work can take him to some odd places, and I've seen some weird things sitting in the back of his car every now and then, but I never asked questions.

And why not? I suddenly wonder. *Why the hell not?*

I'm a lawyer, for Christ's sake. I know better than most the many ways in which people will lie, cheat, and steal in order to get what they want. I'm not saying that Robert is doing any of those things—in fact, it seems like he's the victim in this situation—but that doesn't mean I should go walking into this particular trap like a wide-eyed virgin. I haven't been one of those in a long time.

But being wide-eyed does give me an idea.

"Eye Wide Open Detective—"

I don't give Nico a chance to finish.

"This is Helena Thorne, I just left your office an hour or so ago. I'm calling back because my circumstances have changed."

"Have they?" Nico says, and I can hear him leisurely putting his feet up on his desk. I try not to imagine the smirk forming on his face, as he anticipates me retracting everything that I said earlier, reasserting my faith in my husband, and demanding my deposit back.

"Yes," I say. "I no longer think Robert is cheating on me. However, I still need your assistance and you are free to keep my money."

"I was going to anyway," he says easily. "But please, continue."

I glance at the sun in my passenger seat, mildly put-off by its presence. "You recall that I said my husband likes to dabble in antiques? He also has a passing interest in magical artifacts, and I believe he has stumbled across something that has caused him quite a bit of trouble."

"Oh, really?" Nico asks. "And what makes you think this?"

"Mostly the ransom phone call I just received."

I'm rewarded by a long pause.

"Okay," he admits. "You have my attention." I hear his feet hit the floor and a click as a pen comes out. "What do they want?"

I take a picture of the sun and send it via text.

"I just sent it your way. I can't imagine why it's anything special. It looks to me like something a farmer would hang on their barn for good weather."

"Like a boon?" Nico asks, his voice changing as he puts me on speakerphone so he can see the picture.

"Or a hex," a female voice says. "Hepa here."

"Yes, I remember you. The I.T. girl," I say, my lack of enthusiasm showing in my voice.

"Not just an I.T. girl," she retorts. "I'm a witch. And yes, a real one, not a black-pointy-hat-on-Halloween one. I can make your hair turn gray from here, so you'd be smart to listen to me."

Witch or not, I can't say I'm enjoying her tone. "Ridiculous," I say. "How could you possibly—"

"Check your rearview mirror," she says.

"Seriously? I don't have time—"

"Check. It." Hepa says again, a steel in her voice that I recognize...except it's usually in mine. I sigh, and glance in the rearview mirror, only to see that my blonde locks have gone completely gray.

"Change it back," I say, tightly, my teeth clenched. "Change it back or I'll—"

"What? Sue me?" Hepa laughs, and I can tell she could care less about human threats.

Clearly she's never before met a human who is an actual threat. I guess it's time to properly introduce myself. "No, I wouldn't sue you. I would press charges for assault. Performing witchcraft on unwilling or unwitting people is illegal. And please don't think that you could simply deny it. I would call the man sitting beside you to the stand and he would under oath tell everyone that my hair was a perfect blonde when we met earlier today, then after being clearly threatened by you—it turned gray."

"You're making this up," Hepa says, but I can tell she's starting to worry.

"I assure you, I'm not. Perhaps you should stay more on top of the news. I assume most of you stopped paying attention after supes were given the same protections and rights as humans. However the right to exist without persecution doesn't mean you can trample my rights. I was actually a top consultant when Congress was drawing up the new laws to ensure that supe powers are treated as weapons when they are used as such."

"Gods," Hepa groans. "Fine. I changed your hair back. Just please stop talking at me."

I smile with satisfaction, knowing I've won and resisting the urge to rub it in. Instead I simply say, "I think we understand each other now."

"Yeah, we're both nasty bitches," Hepa says. "I can't say for sure what that thing is riding shotgun, but I can tell you that it's got some powerful vibes. Strong enough that I can pick them up even through that pic you sent Nico."

"Okay," I say, my pulse picking up a notch. "But what do you think it is?"

"There are twelve rays on that sun," Hepa answers. "Can you look closer? Is there anything inscribed on them? Or maybe a symbol?"

I lean over, not relishing being closer to the thing. There's still a smear of my blood where it cut me, and I take the scarf from my hand to wipe it away. Sure enough, some rust rubs away and Hepa is right—there is a small symbol etched into the end of the ray.

"Yes," I tell her. "There is something here. It looks like a...I don't know, maybe fancy letter "n" with a loop at the end?"

"Send a pic," Hepa says. "Humans are bad at words."

Considering that I've heard supes mess up every saying from "caught red-handed" to "having your ass in a sling"— which came out as "had a red hand up his ass with a sling"—I really don't think Hepa has room to criticize humans using our own tongue. But I also don't feel like drawing this out any further. I just want answers, and I want them now.

"Capricorn," Nico says, and Hepa seconds him.

"What?" I ask.

"It's a sign of the zodiac—" Hepa begins.

"Yes, I know that," I snap. "It happens to be my sign."

"Why am I not surprised?" Hepa mutters.

"Anyway," Nico breaks in. "I think Hepa is onto something here. The sun has twelve rays, each one representing a sign of the zodiac."

"Thanks for mansplaining my theory back to me," Hepa says.

"I didn't."

"You did," I cut in. "But can we get to the point?"

"I think it's possible..." He breaks off, and I hear a low muttering as he and Hepa confer about something. My phone vibrates in my hand, and my heart leaps when I see that it's a text from Robert. Of course, I know the kidnappers were going to send the meet-up location, but I still have a moment of bright joy just seeing his name on my screen.

Dammit, I am still in love with this man.

"Helena?" Nico says. "Hepa and I think your husband might have found something quite powerful, something that would definitely make him a target. If this is what I think it is—well, *part* of what I think it is—you could both be in some serious trouble."

"What do you mean, *part*?"

"Hepa and I went to school together," Nico says. "I don't know if you're aware, but there used to be a few magical academies where supes sent their teenage children."

"Yes, I know," I say. "There was even a reality show filmed at the one...what was it? Amazon College?"

"Amazon Academy," Hepa corrects me. "The other two were Underworld Academy—which later became a reformatory for supes deemed criminal—and lastly, where Nico and I went to school. Mount Olympus Academy."

"Right," I say. "I'm familiar."

Robert is a nut for any supe-themed TV show. When The History Channel came out with an educational show about the history of supes, they did an episode on each of the supernatural academies. Robert had taken a keen interest in the Mount Olympus Academy episode...and now I think I know why.

"That one is closed now, right?" I say. "It collapsed. But there was a massive library there, as well as holdings for magical objects, correct?"

"Yes," Nico says, clearly taken aback.

"And you think my husband might have gotten his hands on something that was salvaged from there?"

"I think it's possible. If this is what I think it is, there are three parts to it. When we were in school, it was rumored that Mount Olympus Academy had been a designated holding spot for one of those pieces. It was broken up by the gods as a protective measure."

"Protective how?" I ask.

"I think…" Nico trails off. "It's possible that what you have is a *talentum dei*—an object that can give its wielder the power of a god."

"Oh," I say.

"I don't know if you understand how serious this is," Nico adds when I don't say anything else.

I laugh, the sound cold and metallic in my mouth. "Oh, I understand very well. My husband has stumbled upon an object that men will literally kill for. Assuming he can be safely extracted from his current predicament, there's still the question of whether law enforcement has gotten wind of his involvement. If so, I might lose him, regardless, to a hefty prison sentence. Possessing a magical artifact with intent to wield it is a crime." I close my eyes and let my head rest against my steering wheel, feeling both furious and helpless. But also hurt. Why did Robert not trust me enough to come to me with this? I could have advised him. I could have told him…to run far, far away.

"Helena, are you still there?" Nico asks.

"Yes," I sigh. "Just contemplating how I personally advocated strong laws protecting magical artifacts. I'm sure this isn't the only *talentum dei* floating around. Considering the type of chaos and destruction such a thing could unleash, it seemed prudent to discourage treasure hunters from seeking them out."

"Some folks aren't that easily discouraged," Nico observes.

Yes, that describes Robert to a T. He is a man who gets what he wants. And he wants everything. I always saw us as two peas in a pod with our unflagging focus. But I would never do something so illegal and...immoral.

"I have to bring it," I tell Nico in a quiet voice. "It's my husband's life. But..." I take a deep breath, realizing I'm about to make a vow that I'm not certain I can keep. "I will not allow it to fall into the wrong hands. Especially if the other pieces are in play."

"I get it," Nico says. "There's nothing I wouldn't give if Paige was in the same situation."

"Aw baby, you say the sweetest things." Paige's voice comes through the line. "But let's be honest, the only thing you'd give anyone who touched me is a broken neck."

There's a low growl in answer and then the sound of kissing. I shake my head, unable to believe my bad luck in choosing a P.I. in the first flush of love.

Finally, I say, "I hate to interrupt but the clock is ticking towards my husband's demise and also the release of a potentially dangerous magical artifact upon the world."

"Potential Armageddon in New Jersey and this is the first I'm hearing of it?" Paige asks, laughter in her voice.

"I really don't think this is a time for levity," I say.

"I get it," Paige answers. "But in times like these I've found that it's either laugh or cry." Before I can tell her that I refuse both of those options, she adds, "So what do you need? Tell me and Nico where you need us and we'll have your back."

"It's a kidnapping," Nico interrupts. "Too many people on site will spook them."

"Maybe they need to be spooked," Paige shoots back.

"No," I cut in. "I'm not risking anything that might lead to Robert getting hurt."

"Oh, your husband, I didn't realize," Paige sounds genuinely concerned. "I'm sorry, I just got back from a late cleaning job. A Bacchus Bacchanal. You wouldn't not believe the mess these assholes leave behind. It's unlike anything I've ever seen before—and I've seen a lot. But I guess that's what happens when a god returns as a ghost."

I frown. I've heard a lot, but I'd thought that ghosts had remained in the realm of fiction.

"Listen," Nico interrupts. "This is what I'm thinking. The best I can do for you is send you in with as much knowledge as possible. Forewarned is forearmed, right?"

"Agreed."

"I have a contact at the university who knows a lot about magical objects. He might be able to identify this thing and tell us more."

"Great," I say. "Give me his number."

"Wait," Paige says. "I've never heard of this contact."

"Ummm…" Nico hesitates. "Yeah, that's because he has a propensity to get women in bed before they get to finish their sentences."

"Oh okay, that makes sense," Paige replies. "If he's a good source it'd be terrible to ruin the relationship by killing him."

"What?" I gasp. "Why would Nico kill him?"

"If he tried to get into Paige's pants." Hepa pipes up.

"Or shorts," I can't help but add.

"Or anything." Nico snickers, but then adds in a more serious tone, "He once told me about the time he spent a week at a convent, but the time he left it was the best little whorehouse in Berlin."

"So he's an incubus," I say. "Someone's going to sue his ass someday and I hope that I get to represent them."

"He's not," Nico counters. "I'm not attracted to him at all and incubi affect everyone."

"Hmm," I say, intrigued by this mystery...and still thinking that I could find a way to take this guy down in court. "I'd still like to talk with him."

"I think it's wiser at this point for you to stay in contact with the kidnappers and be ready to move at a moment's notice. I can meet with my source and be back in touch within the hour."

"Deal," I say, remembering the text from Robert waiting on my phone. Since it came through a part of my brain has been focused on it. Even as I've been talking with Nico and crew, the text notification throbs like a tell-tale heart.

Now clicking over to it, I find directions that will lead me to the people who took Robert. I'm one step closer to finding the man I love.

And one step closer to discovering what I'm willing to risk in exchange for his safe return.

9

Crystal

I stare at the text, surprised.

I know this address from my younger days when supes were first getting involved in the human business world. One of my faves was this sweets shop near our house. It turns out that pixies do know how to make the best pixie sticks.

Some of the businesses, though, were a bit more sketchy. Not to be judgmental or anything—I'm a strong believer in to-each-his-own. But this particular place used to be home to some pretty infamous straw parties. They were gatherings where humans willingly opened their veins for vampires, who wandered around with sharp-tipped straws to puncture their new conquests.

I'm pretty sure that place went under a while ago; the human cops had started performing raids in order to infiltrate and shut down supe businesses—usually on trumped up charges. It's awful, but most people had no idea those types of things were going on.

It wasn't until this super shady anti-supe group got raided and all their secrets came out, that people like me realized how much animosity supes faced. Like millions of others across the globe, I marched in the street and demanded change. And it worked. Now there are laws protecting the supes, giving them the same rights as humans. Still, I'm pretty sure that particular business went bottoms up before they could benefit from it.

And, if I'm remembering correctly, the area where this particular wharf is located isn't exactly a must-see location. I toss my phone aside, and it knocks over some amethysts gathered on my nightstand.

"Sorry," I apologize to the powers that be. "I'm just really amped up."

I stare at the giant zodiac ring taking up a foot of space on my bed.

I don't know what to do—but I know what I'm *going* to do. I'm going to act like a lovestruck fool and drive this heavy, bad-juju-vibes, hunk of metal to my new husband. I'm going to save his life, even if it means putting mine in danger.

Harmony might not be my favorite person right now with the way she's inserted herself into my personal journey of discovery, but I'd be a fool to ignore her warnings and predictions. There's no doubt in my mind that something fishy is going to go down on that dock, and I mean to go in prepared.

"Harmony!" I yell down the stairs. "Do you have any garlic charged?"

In any other household, it would be a weird question. Here, it makes perfect sense. "Yes," she calls back. "I set it in the sun this afternoon. But that won't help you!"

"Thanks," I mutter, pulling out my pure linen pantsuit.

Linen carries an energy frequency of 5000 megaHertZ, giving energy to your body as you move. Most people wear it because they think it keeps them cooler in the summer, but the truth is that it revitalizes their bodies through its natural frequencies.

Harmony once tried to explain that to some people on Coney Island once, and almost got arrested. Luckily a friendly witch was nearby and she was kind enough to cast a temporary memory spell on the policeman before he could cuff Harmony. I tried to thank her for intervening, but she said it was the least she could do. Most people just say that and then don't follow up, but this witch backed it up. She gave Harmony a vial of dragonsblood oil, in thanks for trying to bring the good news of fabric frequencies to our people.

And that oil will be perfect for tonight. I tap some out and apply it to my palms, forehead and lower belly, creating a protective sphere of spiritual armor. It doesn't hurt that my pantsuit is dyed haint blue, a color that wards off evil spirits. People paint their porch ceilings this color in the south, because supposedly it keeps mosquitos at bay. Why can't they see that those are just tiny flying vampires, and that the paint hue is called haint blue for a reason?

I grab my pentagram charm made out of black tourmaline. People misunderstand pentagrams all the time, and I've stopped trying to explain that it will actually ward off negative energy. I have to admit that so far in my experience it seems to actually attract it, but maybe that's only the human vibes. The tourmaline should neutralize any harsh magnetic frequencies, so this charm is doing double duty. I intertwine it with the strand of pearls, doubling down on the positivity and integrity. If anybody tries to lie to me while I'm wearing these pearls, I should know!

Next, I grab my sachet of yarrow. I don't have time to spread the herbs inside on the ground to recapture their connection with the earth, but I do crunch it a little bit between my fingers to release the strong, heady scent. The yarrow goes around my belt to promote general safety and well-being. Where we're going, it won't hurt to carry it close to my mace.

Lastly, I pull fistfuls of dried chamomile from the racks in Harmony's kitchen, braiding them into my hair. It should bring inner peace and contentment to me, which is much needed; my hands are shaking as I twist the last bough into my hair.

Harmony comes around the corner and inspects my work.

"Inner peace?" she asks. "You need more chamomile. This is what having a husband does to a woman."

She clucks her tongue and makes a chamomile crown for me, adding a clove of charged garlic every six inches. They dangle around my face, creating a ring of pure energy that will ward off evil.

"Okay, Harmony," I say, stepping back for her inspection. "What do you think?"

"I think you are prepared to take on the powers of hell," she says, her hands on her hips. "But the real problem here is a human man. Take a shower and go to bed, let him handle his own problems."

"I can't do that," I say, shaking my head, the garlic cloves swaying with the movement. "I'm going to save him." I press my hand over my heart. "I'm going to save my husband."

Harmony's eyes stray to the zodiac circle on my bed. "What is this?"

I curl my hands around it as she grabs the other side. "It's a gift from Bobby." I don't tell her the rest of it, but

Harmony can always sense the words held behind my tongue.

"And?" she demands.

I sigh. "It's what he needs back so his kidnappers will release him."

Harmony gives it a tug. "Let me see it."

"No." I grab it with both of my hands and pull it from her, hiding it behind my back like a small child.

"I will return it to you in a moment, I just want to see if the object will speak to me. It's magic. Powerful magic when combined with its other pieces."

I frown and bring the thing in front of me. "There are other matching parts?"

"I'm not sure," Harmony answers, staring hard at the ring. "I can only tell it gives off an echo, as if searching, calling to its missing bits."

"Aww," I stroke my finger along the cool metal. "It's lonely and misses its friends."

"Perhaps," Harmony replies, but she sounds skeptical. She holds out her hands, palms out. "Now let me hold it."

It's a struggle to hand it over. It's like it wants to be with me. I place it in Harmony's hands but when I pull away it takes a chunk of my flesh with it.

"Ouch," I say, dropping the thing firmly into Harmony's hands. My blood got on the ring too, it fills the tiny etchings and turns a yucky brown. "That can't be a good sign," I say, suddenly more worried and wishing Harmony had never seen it.

"Shh," she hushes me. Her hands caress the object. Closing her eyes, she begins to hum a low chant beneath her breath.

Knowing this might take a few minutes, I bandage my cut, then I go to the fridge and make a few hummus and tomato sandwiches. Robert will probably be hungry after I get him back. I'm just wrapping them in some beeswax paper when Harmony snaps back to life.

"I have seen the future," she announces.

I don't bother asking her what she saw. She says there's nothing more deadly than knowing one's destiny.

"Okay," I reply. "Are you feeling better or worse about me going after Bobby?"

Harmony holds the large zodiac ring out to me. "Much better. Tell your husband welcome to the family and..." She smiles in a way that isn't quite nice. "That he will be the making of you."

Huh. This is a way better response to my marriage than I ever hoped to get. I throw my arms around Harmony.

"Thank you," I say. "But I'm not going to tell him that. I'd rather you say it yourself when I bring him home."

Harmony just smiles and pats my cheek. "You should go now. You don't want to be late."

I shake my head, unable to believe she turned so fast from not wanting me to go, to practically pushing me out the door. "It's not time," I say.

She shakes her head. "Your husband's life hangs in the balance and you are ready to go. This is not a time for hesitation. Go now."

I shrug and then grab the sandwiches off the counter. Harmony is probably right as always. And anyway, Bobby did warn me not to be late.

Won't he be surprised when I actually show up early!

10

Maddie

By the time Aden pulls up in front of the store, I've grown comfortable on the back of his bike. Once I got over the fear and the awkwardness of being pressed up against his hard body, I started to enjoy the feeling of the wind whipping past and exhilarating danger of taking a hairpin turn.

I've always been the type to play it safe, and I suppose for most people riding a motorcycle isn't life on the wild side. For me, though, at 43 years of age—this is the craziest thing I've ever done.

Which, now that I think about it...is kind of sad.

Before I can sink into a self-pity mode, I remind myself that I'm about to quickly outdo that motorcycle ride. Dealing with a hostage exchange is definitely a true daredevil activity.

Which reminds me.......I climb off the bike and I look at my phone. A text is there with the address where I need to deliver the globe. Of course, it's on the other side of town. Damn it.

Quickly I text back, Running late! Please don't hurt Bert! I will be there as soon as I can!

"Everything okay?" Aden asks.

"Yes! Thank you! You were so helpful but I have to go now!" I toss the words over my shoulder as I run around the building to the back entrance. In my first bit of good luck, I see that Bert's Tesla is parked around back. So at least I won't have to Uber to the rendezvous point.

Quickly I type the security code into the keypad and enter the building. The familiar dusty scent hits me. It's strangely comforting. Flicking on the lights, I head for the storage room. We have a locked vault where we keep items deemed too valuable to be kept out on the floor.

When Bert brought the globe in a few weeks ago, he insisted it go in the safe. But when I asked for an approximate value so I could enter it in my revenue worksheet, he told me to keep it off the books, that he thought it could be valuable but needed to do more research first.

It seemed a little fishy; Bert usually made sure he knew what he was buying and what he could sell it for. But he said he'd gotten a deal on the globe that was too good to pass up. He promised, though, that he'd offload it if he couldn't find out more information about it. We take pride in the fact that everything in our store is on the up and up. We even provide our customers a thorough provenance for each item. I know Bert would never risk our integrity by dealing in items that might have been stolen.

Or I thought that I knew…

Taking the globe off the shelf, I hold it in my hands. It's pretty. Unlike a globe showing the land masses and oceans that make up Earth, this one is a reflection of the constellations that crown our planet.

"It's lovely, isn't it?" a low male voice asks. I whirl to see Aden standing in the cage doorway.

"How did you get in here?" I demand. I know I closed the door behind me and it locks automatically.

He smiles gently, like he doesn't want to scare me. "It wasn't difficult. I've broken into much higher security places."

I stare at him, wondering who this man really is. But I now know one thing for sure, "You weren't Stephy's date, were you?"

He winces slightly. "Ahh, no. Not exactly. Though she did proposition me. Unfortunately, being at your lovely wedding—"

"Vow renewal ceremony," I automatically correct him.

"Right, that. As I was there on business, I had to turn your lovely sister down."

I feel weirdly crushed by this. Stupidly, I'd let his dimpled smiles and low honeyed voice make me feel special. But he would've wasted no time taking Stephy against the side of a tree, if not for the fact that he had to keep an eye on the sad, middle-aged lady who got stood up at her own party.

And it's clear now why he was watching me. This was all a set up. My van breaking down. Him being oh so conveniently ready to offer me a ride. He's somehow involved in this thing with Bert. I just know it.

I clutch the globe to my chest. "If you're here for the globe, you can't have it."

"I'm sorry my lovely Maddie..." He frowns and shakes his head. "No, I can't subject you to that awful name. Even now when you are looking at me like I'm the worst type of snake." His eyes narrow as he takes me in, his eyes traveling up my body from the tips of my toes, to my indefatigable curls. "Maddie. Madeline. Lynn...Lena," he says at last, the word almost liquid in his mouth. He draws it out so that it almost rhymes with hyena. "Soft. Romantic. Beautiful. Lena is a name that fits you."

Good God, I must be the worst kind of fool, because even knowing that he's playing me, I can't help but like it.

"Don't think you can talk me into giving this to you," I tell him, my voice shaking.

"What if I told you that what you're holding is only one piece of a very dangerous object? The men who have taken your husband are very bad men. Your husband knew this when he chose to do business with them."

"He would never!" I cry.

Aden laughs. "He does all the time. Not with these particular men. But terrible people of all varieties. So long as their money is green."

I shake my head, now truly upset. "You have no idea what you're talking about! This shop has never had customers of that sort."

"Darling Lena." He gives me a pitying look even as his new name for me acts almost like a caress. "Have you not figured out yet that the shop is just a front? The respectable business your husband uses to disguise his more lucrative dealings in the black market."

Tears prick my eyes. I balance the books. I know we sometimes get sudden influxes of cash. They always seemed too good to be true. But I pretended not to notice.

Aden's hand lands on my shoulder and gives it a squeeze. "You must give me this globe. If you take it to exchange it for your husband's life, it will be combined with its other two parts and it will give some very bad men very great powers. I don't think I need to spell out for you why that is a bad thing."

"No," I say softly. "You don't." Slowly I release my hold on the globe. "Take it," I tell him.

He reaches out so that his hands cover mine. "This is probably a bad time to say that I hope we meet again."

I close my eyes. "Please, just go."

The globe is tugged from my grasp and I can hear Aden's footsteps as he starts to walk away. I open my eyes in time to see him exit into the front display room. Grabbing a bottle of spray polish from a nearby shelf, I chase after him.

"Wait!" I call. Aden stops and looks back at me. He's at the front of the store where I just set up a gorgeous crystal glass display. The streetlights from outside illuminate their carved facets.

I hold up the bottle so Aden can see it. "Let me just clean the fingerprints from it. Professional pride and all that," I explain.

He gives me another one of his smiles, this one almost tender, like I am a sweet child he's generous enough to appease. "All right."

I close the distance between us, my legs trembling beneath me. Like a clumsy idiot, right before reaching him, my foot connects with the leg of one of the tables holding the crystal glassware. A gorgeous goblet trembles and then falls to the ground, shattering.

"Crap on a cracker," I hiss and bend to pick it up.

"Leave it," Aden says.

And he's right, this isn't the time, but I hate to leave messes. Quickly, with two fingers I pick up all the large pieces and set them back on the table. On the last one, I grab it in the wrong place and it slices right through the pad of my finger.

"Ouch!" Dropping it, I watch as blood starts to pour out.

Suddenly, Aden's hands on my upper arms, lifting me to my feet. "What have you done to yourself?"

"It's nothing," I tell him. "I'm just a clumsy idiot."

"What a load of horse pucky. Far as I can see, you're perfect. And that right there is your problem. 'Cause perfect is real hard to sustain." Taking an old-fashioned handkerchief from his pocket, he wraps it around my finger. "There now. All better and no harm done."

"Thanks," I say with a small smile, touched despite myself by this small gesture.

"It was nothing."

"I know, but still this is an awful way to repay you," I say. And then before he can reply, I lift the spray bottle and squirt Aden right in the face.

"What?" he coughs and then he can't say anything else. His entire body goes rigid, frozen in place.

I stare, unable to believe that it worked. Bert gave it to me years ago, when the shop first opened and I refused to have a gun. He found me this instead. A magic potion of some sort that will temporarily turn its victim into a statue. I dreaded the thought of using it, but as time passed and the need never arose, I almost forgot that it existed. It was only as Aden was talking that it caught my eye and I remembered.

Now Aden stares back at me, his body locked into place, but his eyes still alive. And wild. I watch as he twitches, clearly fighting the spell.

"Hee-ee-ll-pp," the word croaks from his throat.

I put a hand to his chest, feeling guilty despite knowing I had no choice. "It only lasts a short while," I tell him.

His throat moves as he swallows and I have to resist the urge to touch him there too.

With a shake of my head, I pull the globe from his grasp and step away.

"I'm sorry," I say. "But I don't know you. Maybe the men who want this object will do bad things with it, but what's to say that you wouldn't be just as bad—or worse?" I look down at the globe unable to continue looking into Aden's desperate eyes. "Anyway, it's my husband's life. He needs me. And I...I need him."

With that I turn on my heel, leaving Aden behind. It's only difficult because he's clearly in pain from the spell. Bert promised it wouldn't hurt anyone...but I'm starting to wonder how much Bert's promises were worth.

It doesn't matter, though. Even if we didn't renew our vows today, the ones from twenty-five years ago still stand.

Bert is the man I vowed to love and cherish. To serve and protect.

'Til death do us part.

11

Helena

I'm headed towards the address that was texted to me —an abandoned wharf in a part of town where a defense lawyer can make a living—when a call comes through from an unidentified number. Normally, I let these go to voicemail, but since I'm suddenly in charge of some sort of rescue operation, I answer it.

"Helena Thorne?" a man's voice asks.

"Speaking," I say, hoping there's just the right amount of venom in my voice, in case this is in fact, Robert's kidnapper.

"This is Ford. I'm an antiquities professor at—"

"Oh yes," I say, remembering Nico's informant. "I hear you're quite the womanizer."

"And I hear you're a Capricorn," he says, without missing a beat.

"I don't really know that it's something I need to apologize for," I say, stiffly.

"Definitely a Capricorn then," he says, and I resist the

urge to hang up on his smugness. I remind myself to Google him later. If there's any hint of him seducing students I'll do a pro bono case against this jerk.

"Do you have any useful information for me?" I ask. "Because I'm about to engage in some criminal activities and I need to prepare."

"Yes, actually," Ford says, suddenly very professorial. "I believe that Mr. Tralano was right about the item you possess. I think it's part of a *talentum dei.* And I'm strongly advising you to throw it into the ocean, as soon as you can."

"I'm sorry, that's not possible," I say. "I can't go into detail but—"

"You need it to ransom your husband," Ford finishes and my hands tighten on the steering wheel.

"Whatever happened to client confidentiality?" I snap.

"Nico only told me what he thought was pertinent," Ford says. "Which is to say that he was discreet. However, I then called back and got Hepa on the line."

"That little—"

"Careful," Nelson says. "She's got tricks that could turn your hair gray."

"Literally. Yes, I know," I interrupt.

"Does your husband often deal in these types of magical objects? It's a dangerous trade. It usually attracts ne'er-do-wells and loners with nothing to lose except their lives. But a man with a wife and even a child..."

"He would never put me or our daughter at risk," I answer between clenched teeth, unable to believe this judgmental ass. "He's had an antique hobby since I've known him and it's always been quite benign. I'm sure he got mixed up in all this quite by accident."

I'm not sure of any such thing, but a wife can't be compelled to testify against her husband.

"Furthermore," I say, "I can't help but think you might be describing yourself when you speak of ne'er-do-wells and losers."

"Loners," he corrects in a voice full of laughter. "And you definitely got my number. But when I'm hunting magical objects it's to keep them out of the hands of men like your husband."

"I told you, I'm sure he never realized what he had."

"Right, right," he agrees in this condescending tone that's the verbal equivalent of a pat on the head. "Look, if you won't throw it in the ocean, then my advice is to make excuses for why you can't come tonight. I'm pretty sure the blood moon up in the sky is the reason for the kidnappers' urgency. Put them off until tomorrow morning. Say you have car trouble or the stomach flu. Hell, you could turn off your phone and just let them twist in the wind and wonder."

"Are you insane? I'm not gambling my husband's life like that. And to be honest, I'm not really interested in your advice. I'm sure this is difficult for a love 'em and leave 'em loner like yourself to understand, but I love my husband and I will do whatever it takes to get him back. If I have to give the Devil the Shroud of Turin, I will."

A low whistle erupts from the phone. "Damn, girl. You sure there's no Leo in there?"

"You have no idea what's inside of me," I taunt.

His low deep laugh comes through the line. "I know what I'd like to put inside you."

I flush—with anger, of course. "You couldn't handle me."

"Mm, that sort of challenge is like waving a red cape in front of a bull."

Now it's my turn to laugh. "That's a well-chosen analogy, because bullfights rarely end well for the bull."

"That's true," Ford admits, "But when one is rules by

deep passions and the unending urge to thrust himself into his opponent—"

"Is everything a double entendre with you?" I interrupt.

Instead of answering my question, his voice drops to a lower more intimate level, "I like sparring with you. I believe you truly would be a challenge."

"You'll never find out," I tell him and then hang up the phone before he can say anything else. The truth is that I love this type of verbal fencing, matching my wits against a mind nearly as sharp as my own. But this isn't the time for it and anyway Ford is too arrogant for my tastes. Although it would be fun to take him down a few pegs...

I push that thought aside and focus on the task at hand. Finding Robert.

I'm driving through a seedy warehouse district now. Half the street lights are out, and the only person I see on the sidewalk is barely making headway in six-inch heels and a staggering gait. New to criminal enterprises, I pull up next to her, wondering if the prostitute act is some sort of cover.

It's definitely not. When she hears the approaching engine she turns her head, hopeful for a trick. It's a methed-out harpy, a supernatural species that landed in the real world with a resounding face plant. Harpies are unattractive to begin with—bat-like and wrinkly-skinned, with tiny inverted ears and creepy, membraned wings. Add meth to the mix and things get worse. Put it in a sexy getup and it looks like a marketing campaign for abstinence.

I gas it, and surge past her, finding an empty parking spot near the warehouse. There's no one else around, and I have no further instructions. I double check the address and try to send a text to Robert.

I'm here. I've brought it.

It doesn't go through. Either his battery died, or Robert

did. Shit, I can't think that way. My nerves are already singing and my hands are twitchy. Besides, the kidnappers wouldn't go through all of this trouble to bring me here and then just off my husband before they got what they wanted out of the deal.

I put my head on the steering wheel, and take deep breaths.

I am going to get through this. I am going to save my husband. We are going to be happy again. I will never take what we have for granted. I am literally going to trade the sun for him. I exhale just as another pair of headlights sweeps the warehouse, followed by a second car. I jam my cell into my pocket and get out of the car, hauling the sun out behind me, careful to hold it by the scarf tied around the Capricorn ray. I don't need to lose a finger and bleed out down here. Joel would have his hands full trying to put a positive spin on that.

I face the two vehicles that have pulled into the lot, the sun out in front of me. I hope my face looks right. I hope I look fierce, and loyal, and loving, and all the things that I can and will be, once I have Robert back. But mostly, I want them to see that I've brought it.

The driver's side of one of the cars—a shiny Tesla—clicks open, and a woman wearing an old-fashioned wedding dress steps out, hauling a piece of metal behind her. The driver of the second car—a bright yellow Kia Soul with pink plastic eyelashes on the headlights—gets out next. She's wearing a pantsuit bright enough to blind Liberace, has a bushel of flowers in her crazily braided hair, and bulbs of garlic dangle around her face. She also pulls a piece of metal from her car, keeping it away from her body like it might have been reclaimed from Chernobyl.

The two women look at each other, then at me.

"Give me back my husband!" all three of us say at the same time.

12

———

Crystal

I stare at the other two women. One holds a giant golden sun, the other a bronze globe. I look at my giant zodiac ring.

"I think we're here for the same reason. My husband has a business in magical items."

"Mine too," the one woman says.

"Mine's a hobbyist," the other woman adds. She's the one dressed like a professional, with a dove gray business suit and expensive shoes. She has an aura about her that's so strong, I bet Harmony could see it from miles away. "You a lawyer?" I ask.

"How did you...look, that's not the point." Her words are crisp and impatient, like she's got places to go and people to see. "Our husbands must know each other."

"Yes, they must have each procured a part of the item that whoever kidnapped them wants," the other woman says. Giving us a strained smile, she adds, "I'm Maddie."

I look at her. She's got oodles of gorgeous black hair,

streaked a bit with gray. It suits her. She's also wearing a wedding dress.

"Did you just get married, Maddie?" I ask. "Because I just did too! Yesterday."

"No, I've been married for twenty-five years," she tells me with a sort of sad smile on her face. I get the feeling that maybe it's a sore subject.

"Sorry. You *are* wearing a wedding dress. I'm Crystal, by the way."

"Hi Crystal, I'd say it's nice to meet you, but in these circumstances..." She laughs in a way that sounds a little unhinged. "Look, I have got to get this to whoever wants it," she adds desperately. "I was supposed to be here at eleven but it's nearly midnight."

"Well, I'm early," I tell her, "so I guess it all balances out."

"No," the lawyer woman interrupts. "That's not how time works."

"Time doesn't work at all," I gently correct her. "It just is. Like an invisible current." I sway a little to give her a visual, but she just stares at me in that narrow-eyed way that some people have. I don't hold it against her. Harmony always says we need to have compassion for the non-believers, they go through the world closed off to so many of its wonders. So I just say, "You didn't tell us your name."

She purses her lips like she might hold it back, but then says, "Helena. Now can we stop wasting time?"

"Sure. Why don't we all go in together?" I say. "Let's rescue our husbands."

We walk awkwardly toward the building but the door won't budge so we make our way around the side. I feel safe with all my charms jingling, but Maddie's wedding dress is getting all dirty. Helena looks beyond put out, but I can't tell if it's because her husband got kidnapped or because she's ruining her heels.

"I'm glad you two are here," I tell Helena and Maddie. "It's a little less scary with all three of us together."

Maddie gives me a smile. "I hope our husbands have found comfort in each other's company too."

"Shh," Helena hisses at us. It's pretty clear that she's the killjoy in the group.

I don't believe in letting my happiness be squashed, though, so I just ignore her and say to Maddie, "My Bobby makes friends everywhere he goes. I'm sure he is best buddies with your two hubbies by now."

Helena comes to such a swift stop that I bump into the back of her. Hands on her hips, she spins to face me, her eyes eerily intense in the moonlight. "What did you just say?"

I roll my eyes. "Okay, I get it. I'm being too loud." I mime zipping my lips. "Better?"

Maddie gently touches my arm to get my attention. Looking her way, I see that she's got a sick expression on her face. Like she might be about to toss her cookies kind of sick. "I think she wanted you to repeat the part when you mentioned your husband's name," she says.

I frown at the two of them because even for people I barely know, I can tell they're acting weird. "My husband is Bobby Thorne, Antiquarian Expert." I grin at them, trying to lighten the mood a little. We can't save our husbands while swimming in bad energy. "That's what it says on his business card, but after the honeymoon we had this past weekend, I told him he should maybe consider adding, *Tantric Sex Master*." I giggle. "The orgasms I had were seriously intense."

Maddie's face goes gray. She swivels away from me and barfs into a nearby row of bushes.

"I'm sorry," I say. "Was that TMI?" I look to Helena hoping she might help, but her face is twisted like she might be the next to blow chunks. "I didn't mean to overshare, but at the same time, this seems like an overreaction. Sex is a natural and beautiful act."

"It's not that," Helena tells me, her lips tight. "I'm upset because my husband is Robert Thorne." She gestures to Maddie, who's wiping her mouth. "And I think that's her husband's name as well."

"Bert Thorne," Maddie groans.

"Wow," I say. "That is so amazing. I saw a documentary about something just like that. These triplets were separated at birth and raised by different families, but then by happenstance they found each other later in life." I smile at the two other women who weirdly don't seem to get how cool this is. "Our husbands are all brothers!"

Helena looks at Maddie. "Should I tell her, or do you want to?"

Maddie shrugs. "Just be nice."

"What are you two talking about?" I demand.

Helena sighs and then takes out her phone. After turning it on, she holds it out to me. "This is my husband." There's a picture of Helena and a man who looks just like my Bobby with an arm around her shoulders.

I clap my hands. "They're identical triplets! Wow! The resemblance is uncanny!"

"That's because this is your Bobby," Helena says, her voice flat.

Maddie peers around me to see the picture. "And my Bert," she adds.

A sickening feeling is growing in my stomach. But I

refuse to believe it. I don't want to. I feel like all my charms and gems and preparation are for nothing.

I gulp and force myself to say the words. "Are you saying we're all married to the same man?"

A sob escapes Maddie. "We have four kids together."

"He and I have a daughter," Helena's voice is icy cold as she shares this.

Suddenly I understand why Maddie threw up. "Do you have any dogs?" I ask. I know it's silly but Bobby promised we'd get a puppy together. It felt so special, like a fluffy, furry promise.

"A basset hound named Ava," Helena tells me.

I sniffle as tears fill my eyes. This is the final betrayal. "Is that short for avocado? Bobby just loves avocados."

"Why would Ava be short for avocado?" Helena screeches, finally showing some emotion. "Ava is short for Ava. It's a popular name." She throws up her hands. "I can understand her—" Helena points at Maddie. "Twenty-five years, you said, right?" She doesn't wait for Maddie to respond before continuing, "He clearly married you when the two of you were both too young to know better. Then years later he met me, realized how much better we suited one another, but he couldn't bring himself to leave you and the four kids. I mean, I'd bet money that you're some sort of housewife," Helena says, a sneer in her voice.

"Go fuck yourself," Maddie says to her. Which I think maybe means that, yes, she is a housewife? I don't know why Helena acts like that's such a bad thing. Raising kids and keeping house is a lot of work. Before I can make that point out loud, Helena has swung to face me.

"But what could he have seen in you?" She looks me up and down, like she's trying to strip me to my skin and even under that too. "You're not a hot young twenty-something—"

"Bobby and I celebrated my fortieth this past weekend," I tell her, head high. No way am I just going to stand her and let her monologue without getting a few words in.

"Oh wow, a wedding and a birthday. What a big weekend for the two of you," Helena snaps. And then all at once her face crumbles. Covering it with her hands, she sobs, "I thought he loved me."

I can't stand to see another person suffer. "I'm certain he does," I tell her. And I believe it too. I trust my instincts and I know when Bobby said "I do" to me this past weekend that it was with love and nothing else. "I'm pretty sure he loves us all."

"I think you're right," Maddie says in a quiet defeated voice. "He loves all of us...but just not so much that one of us is enough for him."

"That's because nothing is ever enough for him," Helena adds, her sobs having tapered off.

The three of us stand in silence considering this, and come to the same conclusion. We married a bottomless pit of a man and right now all of us are hurtling through the darkest part of it.

13

———

Maddie

"Stop!" a shady figure orders as the three of us approach the open door leading into the warehouse.

We debated turning back and leaving Bert/Robert/Bobby to his fate. But I think we all knew that having come this far, we were going to finish it. And then maybe finish him. The man with the gun is standing over Bert, who has a black eye and a trail of blood running from the corner of his mouth. Despite myself, my heart squeezes for him.

Another figure joins the man, a slight woman holding a very large gun.

"Stop right there," she says to us, which is basically a repeat of what the man already said. And we haven't moved an inch since then. I have the feeling that perhaps these two aren't quite professionals in the kidnapping game.

"What are they all doing here together?" Bert snarls at

the two people with guns. He talks to them like they're his lackies. "I told you to space them out."

The man casually kicks Bert's back. "Your personal problems aren't our concern."

"Hey!" I snap, stepping forward. "We did what you said, we brought the objects, so let him go."

I watch as Bert's gaze flickers from me to Helena to Crystal, as he tries to deduce if we figured out his deception yet. Finally, he must decide to play it safe, because he says, "Thank you for coming. All of you."

"Of course we came," Helena says. "What sort of w..." She takes her time forming the w and I watch as Bert tenses, expecting the gig to be up. But instead of *wife*, she finishes with, "Women wouldn't?"

I almost want to high five her despite that earlier housewife comment. I bet she could spend days letting Bert swing, wondering if he got away with it or if the whole thing is blown.

Unfortunately, we don't have that kind of time.

"Assemble the item," the woman orders.

"Tell us what is going on," Helena demands. Her voice is iron, like she's used to giving orders and having them followed. That must be nice. Too many years as a mom has made me more of the type that's used to giving orders and having the people on the receiving end of them pretend to suffer from hearing loss.

"Look," the woman with the gun says. "No one needs to get hurt."

"They're lying!" Bert yells. "They need a sacrifice!"

"We only need one," the woman says. "My brother is sick. He has cancer. This idiot"—she kicks Bert and this time I don't object—"is the only one who has to get hurt."

I look at the woman's brother and he seems off. His skin

is a sickly gray. "I'm sorry your brother is sick," I say to the woman. "But does he want to have his life saved at the expense of someone else's life?"

The brother answers, "It doesn't really bother me. Especially since this dude's a piece of shit."

Okay, well, he's got me there.

"You can't kill Bobby," Crystal bursts out. "I can't give my mother the satisfaction."

"Let him go and you can have the artifact," Helena says. I don't know how she can summon the steel in her voice. My spine feels like rubber.

"I need the *talentum dei* assembled while the blood moon is full," the man says. His voice is harsh, and he lets out a ragged cough. "Hurry."

The woman walks forward brandishing her gun. "Do it. Now. I will kill all of you to save my brother."

"Okay, we're doing what you say." I put the globe on the ground in front of us. I've done enough DIY projects that I can figure it out. "Helena, that sun looks like it fits into the circle that Crystal is carrying."

Helena places it inside, where it clicks into place. But there's nothing holding it as it floats in the middle. Magic. I don't have time to think about it, though, as Crystal hefts it into my arms. I ask them each to hold open a hemisphere and I place the circle inside. That's it—all three pieces are in place.

"Woah," Crystal breathes. "I can feel the power coming from it."

Weirdly, I can too. It's almost like an electrical current, lifting the hair on my arms. I can't help remembering Aden's words about someone being able to cause destruction with this. Sure, right now she just wants to save her brother, but what happens then? Will he be a healthy normal person or will he become some sort of superpowered maniac? I hate to say it, but the way he so casually dismissed Bert's life makes me think he doesn't have a well-developed sense of morality.

"Like I said, we only need one sacrifice to save my brother. Turn around and leave," the woman tells us, her gun pointed right at me. Her brother eagerly steps forward, arms outstretched like he can't wait to get his hands on the object. I want to back away, but Helena and Crystal hold their ground.

"This isn't a healing device," Helena says. "Why did you choose it, of all things?"

The woman frowns. "Yes, it is." She looks down at Robert. "You told us this was our best bet."

He shrugs and gives one of his famous devil-may-care smiles. "What can I say? I had plans for this baby tonight. When you two got in the way, I simply let you do some of the work for me."

There's a loud bang and the woman with the gun falls down dead.

Beside me Crystal screams and Helena curses. But I'm struck dumb, watching as Robert pulls a small gun from his pocket and aims it at the dead woman's brother.

He just took her life so easily, like it was nothing. Before I can yell out a warning, he shoots the man in the back. He falls forward, stumbling into my arms.

"Robert Thorne!" I yell.

I recognize the tone of my voice. It's the same one I use when one of the boys walks through the house with muddy shoes. It's my "you know better than that" voice. Except this is way beyond muddy shoes. He just murdered someone in cold blood. The man I've slept beside and raised children with and who comforted me when the baby bunnies I tried to rescue didn't make it.

I thought I'd married a man who might at times be a bit selfish and self-involved, but who at heart was good, kind, and loving.

Well, the loving part was right. He's real good at loving.

Bert takes the man from me and tosses him aside like he's trash. "Sorry about that, Maddie," he says. His finger touches the front of my dress where fresh blood covers it. "I'll get you a new dress."

"It was for the vow renewal ceremony," I tell him, dazed by his nonchalance. Like my dress getting blood on it is the problem here.

His eyes widen and he slaps a hand against his forehead. "Damn it! Getting kidnapped didn't just ruin my day, did it? It affected you, too. I'm so sorry, baby!"

I stare at him, in shock but also resignation. This is the man I married. It's who he's always been. For the first time in my life, I'm seeing him clearly.

What an idiot I've been.

"I'll make it up to you," he says now, which is what Bert always says.

I shake my head at him as my throat closes up. "I don't think you can this time."

"You owe her a lot more than a do-over," Helena says. She has the woman's gun and is pointing it straight at Bert. "In fact, you owe all of your wives a lot more."

He grins in a you-got-me kind of way, and a soft sigh escapes him. He walks toward her until the gun is pressed against his heart. "Pull the trigger if you must. But I'd prefer you go home." Bert glances my way and then to Crystal, including us. "All three of you go home. I've got to clean up here and then…"

"And then what?" I ask. "Which one of us gets you afterward? Should we draw straws?"

An alarm on Bert's watch goes off. He looks down at it and curses softly. "We can't do this right now." Turning away from us, he reaches down for the man he shot. I think maybe he's going to try and save him, but instead Bert just dips his fingers into the blood flowing from the man's body and then wipes it across the globe, murmuring an incantation as he does so.

The globe begins to spin. I put my hands on either side of my head, which also feels like its spinning. What was it that Aden said about this? It can grant great power and destruction...and Bert is the one who wants it.

"Ladies, you don't want to be here for this," Bert warns.

"Oh, crap, my mother was right," Crystal cries.

"I'm not going anywhere," Helena says, still holding the gun. "Now get away from that so I can shoot you."

A brilliant red light shoots from the whirling device, up to the sky. The moon becomes bright as the sun and a red beam hits me. I try to sidestep away, but the beam follows me like a spotlight. Marking me.

Not just me, Helena and Crystal too.

Bert stares at the beams and then at his own hands, wreathed in darkness. "No," he yells at the globe. "Not them. Me! Choose me!"

He reaches into the light, trying to turn off the device. It consumes him, lighting him up from the inside out, like a fire. Bert screams in agony.

I join his scream as I'm lifted off my feet, then the light goes out and I crash down onto the soggy wood of the wharf.

Shakily I get to my feet. Crystal and Helena do the same. Bert comes to my shoulder.

"Well, that didn't go the way I planned," he says.

I round on him, not sure if I want to hit him or hug him. But something's wrong. I can see right through him. I reach out a hand and it passes through his chest. I look to the ground where he also lays. No, not him. His body.

"Too late, to kiss, kill, or fuck me," he says. "I'm already dead."

I stare at the women around me. Crystal and Helena.

I'm so mad that the anger is a hot wave through my body. A rush of air surrounds me, lifting up the skirt of my dress. I again lift into the air as the wind screams across the open water.

"Um...guys?" Crystal calls. She has a similar tornado around her, but hers is formed of water. I look to Helena, who has the dirt and muck of the wharf surrounding her.

I don't know why, but I walk to them, but feet propelling me through the air. As soon as the vortex of our elements meet, we're caught up in the whirl. I don't want to but I hold out my hand to steady myself and catch each of theirs in mine. Once we're holding hands the maelstrom quiets. As one, we sink gently down to the ground.

I look at these women with whom I have shared my husband for who knows how many years. It would be easy to hate them. And myself too. For not being enough for Bert.

But I know who deserves my anger.

I turn on the ghost of my husband. "You had better start talking or I'm going to ghostbust your ass."

THE END

———

Get more of Maddie's story! Pre-order Powers of the Zodiac Book 1: The Midlife Gemini's Guide to a Bad Horoscope - available wherever books are sold! Keep reading for a sneak peek!

Want to know about all the latest releases? Sign up for the Marley Lynn's Newsletter! When you sign up you'll receive **THREE FREE SHORT STORIES**—all set in the Mythverse!

THE MIDLIFE GEMINI'S GUIDE TO A BAD HOROSCOPE SNEAK PEAK

Feeding your dead husband to a Hydra on the Jersey Shore should be like a solitary experience. But here at last is the upside to discovering my husband is—er, *was*—a polygamist. I've got his two other wives, Helena and Crystal, here to help me.

I know, so far as silver linings go, it's a stretch. But my life in the course of a day went from Pinterest perfect to darkest timeline—so I think it's okay.

"Darkest timeline," I whisper under my breath and then start to laugh, a little bit hysterically.

"Pull it together!" Helena snaps. "We still have to get him in the water."

Right. I heave up my end of our shared dead husband. Helena and Crystal each take one of his shoulders, leaving me with the feet.

"On three," Helena orders with authority, like she disposes of dead bodies all the time. "One, two...THREE!"

As one we fling Bert into the brackish water. He hits it with a splash and disappears, then floats back up to the top, bobbing face down.

Somehow I'm left holding one of his shoes. "Oh," I say stupidly, recognizing it as a pair I bought him for his last birthday. He likes the ones with the memory foam soles because he's on his feet a lot.

Helena snatches it from my hands and tosses it into the water. "No keepsakes. No evidence," she says, like it's her personal mantra. Maybe it is.

"It's just a shoe..." I say.

"Haven't you ever seen CSI?" Crystal asks me. "The other half of the pair is on his dead body. Use your head, before you lose it."

"We're not going to take any chances here," Helena snaps. She'd taken all of his things out of his pockets, thinking ahead. I admire her, but she also unnerves me with her calm, quiet strength.

We stand watching our husband's floating corpse. It's a dark night; the full moon keeps disappearing behind the clouds.

"How long will it take the Hydra..." I trail off.

"Nico said not long, and that we can't miss it," Helena answers tersely. Nico is her private eye (who happens to have only one eye) who gave us the idea of disposing of Bert's body this way. He says the mob has kept this particular Hydra well fed for years and he knows the routine.

We stand silently. Waiting and awkward in the way of strangers.

Crystal breaks the silence. "I've been meaning to tell you, Maddie, I just love your dress." Her eyes shine at me with warmth and sincerity.

I gulp and look back at Helena, realizing that I prefer her cold hard stare. It makes me feel less bad about hating her.

"Thanks," I say to Crystal. Looking down at the dress, I

gather the dirty, blood-spattered skirt in my hands.

"Today was mine and Bert's vow renewal ceremony." With those words my throat thickens and tears cloud my vision.

Bert ended up being a no-show at the ceremony. It's not the first time he missed an event, but never one of this magnitude. Even though I thought he'd gotten caught up on a business trip, I still couldn't help but feel hurt and betrayed. Yet I also had known that he would be full of profuse apologies, extravagant forgive me gifts, and promises to make it up to me.

At least that's how it had always gone in the past. Instead, I found out what true hurt and betrayal feels like.

A rough sob bursts out of me, bending me in half so that I have to press my fists to my thighs to stay standing. Suddenly a hand grips my face, pulling me upright again.

It's Helena. "Save the breakdown for later. When we are not standing at the spot where we have just disposed of our husband's body." She releases me and I quickly take a step back.

"Ow..." I rub my face. "That wasn't necessary."

"Don't lose your shit and I won't have to manhandle you," she tells me.

"We can't all be an ice queen," I retort. We glare at each other.

"Um, girls...I think it's happening," Crystal tells us.

We scramble back from the shore as the hulking beast comes near, the dark waters spreading in a V-shape as the massive back breaks the surface, approaching Bert's dead body. A few sickening bites and my husband is gone. There's something poetic about Bert's three wives watching him be devoured by a three-headed Hydra. The beast lifts its heads above water, eyes us, then gives us a nod. Kind of like, *thanks for the snack!* It lets out a belch and then with a gigantic splash, disappears back beneath the water.

We each react in our own way.

I sink to my knees, emotionally blown. Helena smacks her hands together, like she's cleaning them of the whole situation. Crystal takes a step backward and mutters, "I do not claim any negative energy from this experience."

We're all so different. How could Bert truly love all three of us?

"So what exactly are we to each other?" I ask.

"Sister wives!" Crystal offers.

"Bigamy Bitches," Helena counters. "Actually, strike that from the record. We're nothing to each other. The one thing that connects us is currently being digested."

"But we saw his ghost," Crystal says in a tiny voice.

"For only a minute," I cut in. "And then he disappeared. He probably went into the light."

Helena snorts. "Only if the light leads to hell." She scrubs a hand over her face. "Speaking of hell, what the hell time is it?"

"Time for a drink!" Crystal says. "It is definitely a double apple schnapps night."

Helena and I stare at Crystal. You'd think she was half of our age, but we're all over forty.

"Fine," Helena says at last. "I could drink."

"Yaaassss," Crystal looks at me. "You in?"

"Why the heck not," I say. I'm not a huge drinker, but finding out that your husband is married to two other women, and then having to dispose of his body with those women, is an occasion for drinking.

It's not like we killed him or anything. Although he would've deserved it. That's the reason why Helena insisted that going through the authorities would be a bad move.

"Look at the situation," she said. "No one will believe we didn't kill him. *I* can't believe we didn't kill him."

She had a really good point. And I can't take even the chance of me going to jail. I agreed, as did Crystal. Instead of calling 911, Helena called Nico, her personal private eye. Luckily, he and his girlfriend showed up right away.

Nico, I quickly discovered, was a handsome, but also dangerous-looking, werewolf with an eyepatch. I would not like to get on his bad side. I can imagine that getting on his good side must be interesting...I'm tempted to take his girlfriend aside and advise her to 'lock that down', but after tonight I have a lot less faith in the bonds of marriage. The girlfriend, Paige, doesn't really look like the type to appreciate unsolicited advice anyway. Unlike Nico, she's just a normal human, but projects a 'mess with me at your own peril' type of vibe.

They immediately took charge. Nico separated us and then one by one asked us to explain what happened. Meanwhile, Paige pulled some sort of bone out of her back pocket, explaining to us that it was a magical talisman that gave her the ability to communicate with animals.

"I've had an interesting life," she said, offhandedly, and started talking to the birds in the rafters of the warehouse where everything went down. I guess between Nico comparing our stories and whatever Paige learned from the birds—they believed we were telling the truth.

And the truth was this—we'd each come to this warehouse on the seedy end of town to save our husbands who had been kidnapped and held for ransom.

My husband of twenty-five years, Bert.

Helena's beloved Robert.

And finally Crystal who just this weekend had married her Bobby.

It was only when we showed up that we realized there was only one husband. And he'd married all three of us.

Helena, the high-powered lawyer.

Crystal, a woo-woo hippie type.

And me, plain old Maddie, the high school sweetheart.

Each of us had gotten the same message. Bert, Robert, Bobby was in trouble. He'd been kidnapped and was being held for ransom. The people holding Bert wanted an antique that he had split into three parts and given to each of us. He gave me the hefty bronze globe. Crystal was given a huge ring of metal that fit around the globe and had all the zodiac signs etched around the circle. Helena had the base, a large golden sun.

Armed with these objects, we went to rescue our husband from his kidnappers. In the moments that followed things went a little crazy. When put together, the three artifacts became one, called the *talentum dei*—an object that can give its wielder the power of a god—which had been part of Bert's plan, apparently.

But the *talentum dei* didn't choose him.

It chose us. The wives.

I remember a bright red light and being lifted off my feet. It felt like I was in the eye of a hurricane. Crystal and Helena were each floating as well. Crystal was surrounded in a geyser of water and Helena in a cyclone of sand and dirt. For a moment, its power filled the three of us. For whatever reason, we were able to withstand it. But Bert did not. He was struck instantly dead when he tried to touch the *talentum*. When we crashed back to the soggy wharf I realized the kidnappers and Bert were dead, but we...we were alive.

"Wow," Paige said, when she had heard our whole story. "And I thought my ex was a piece of work."

"He is a piece of work," Nico replied in a low growl. With one arm he reached out and snagged Paige, pulling her tight against his side.

Watching them, my heart gave a little squeeze of pain. The two of them were clearly in love. They didn't need to say anything—anyone with eyes could see it.

I'd once thought that Bert and I were that type of couple too. But I'd been wrong about a lot of things.

"Here's what I think," Nico said, breaking into my thoughts. "Leave the kidnappers here and let the cops sort out what happened to them. Take the *talentum*, split it up again and hide it as best as you can. As for…" Nico's gaze landed on Bert's body slumped on the dirty cement floor.

"Bert," I say at the same moment that Crystal says, "Bobby" and Helena says, "Shitbag."

"Right…him," Nico says. "If you want to get rid of him, I got an idea. But you'll have to take care of it yourselves. Body disposal is not in my job description."

"It's true," Paige adds. "He gets pissy when you ask him to take care of a body. I once had a dead vamp on my porch that was left as a gift from VSK…that's the vampire serial killer, you probably remember he was in the news quite a bit." We all nodded. "I called Nico and he sniffs the body a few times—"

"I did more than sniff him," Nico interrupts.

"Right, but you definitely got his scent, because you went on and on about it—"

"I'm a werewolf! We're known for our incredible noses. It's like having access to a whole separate world that everyone else is blind to. And it's also why you can't just switch laundry detergents without telling me—"

"It was on sale—"

"There are some things you don't buy on sale."

"Hey!" Helena snaps. "If I'm paying by the hour, this fight needs to happen on your own time."

Paige and Nico exchange chagrined glances.

"Sorry," she says.

"Don't worry," Crystal breaks in. "You guys are such a cute couple. My Bobby and I are the same…" She trails off and her face loses color as she realizes. "Oh."

I understand where she's coming from. Even with Bert's body in front of us, it didn't feel quite real that he was dead. And now, even after listening to a monster consume him, it still feels like someone else's nightmare.

"This place," Helena tells us, her finger pointing to a high-end establishment.

"Umm, isn't this a private club?" I ask. When we talked about drinks I was thinking more along the lines of grabbing a few bottles of Two Buck Chuck.

"Yes, it is," Helena replies. "And I'm a member."

Crystal shrugs when I look her way, so I follow the two of them inside. Overhead a giant chandelier glisten, and plush booths set along dark paneled walls make it clear that this is a nice place. I'm worried about cost, but Helena leads us to a bar, pulls out her platinum credit card, and orders a bottle of five-hundred-dollar whiskey like she would ask for a rum and coke.

I can't believe it.

"Bring it to our table," Helena orders and then turning on her heel, strides toward an empty booth in a dark corner. When the bottle arrives, Helena pours. I'm not really a whiskey drinker. I prefer a nice wine spritzer but I'm not about to mention that to either of them.

Bringing the drink to my nose, I give an experimental sniff. The fumes bring tears to my eyes and singe my nose hairs.

Helena raises her glass. "A toast!" she declares, her teeth bared in what I think is meant to be a smile. "This is the one my father loved and that Robert and I then made our own..." She hesitates and has to swallow as a telltale wetness enters her eyes. "Here's to you and yours. And to mine and ours. And if mine and ours ever come across your and yours, I hope you and yours will do as much for mine and ours, as mine and ours have done for you and yours."

Without waiting for Crystal and me to clink her glass, Helena tips her back and drains it. I take a tiny sip and immediately start coughing as it burns the whole way down.

"I like that," Crystal says, after taking a drink of her own whiskey. "But we're kinda the you and yours to each other, but also the mine and ours. I mean, we're all tangled up now."

She's right. I realize. Bert's bigamy affects more than just the three of us at this table.

"Do you have kids?" I ask suddenly. "Do my kids have half-siblings they've never met?"

"I have a daughter," Helena says. "She's fifteen."

"Ollie's also fifteen!" I exclaim, momentarily excited. Then I realize that she and I were pregnant at the same time. Bert was rubbing her belly and then coming home to rub mine. I mean, I know he did worse with her than rub bellies, but dreaming about our baby to come always felt so special and intimate. "I also have an older boy, and a twin boy and girl," I add.

"Wow, that's a brood," Crystal says.

Helena is seething. "I can't believe the bastard..." she says under her breath. "Four secret kids." I'm guessing she's thinking about belly rubbing too.

I look at Crystal, who knocks back her whiskey and lets out a long breath. "And you?"

"Me, oh no," she says. "I don't have any kids. It never interested me. I thought Bobby was great because we both didn't want kids..."

I can't decide which is worse, the child he has with Helena or the fact that he denied having any children to Crystal. Somehow the latter makes me even more mad. I didn't really have a chance to decide if I was interested in having kids or not. It just happened.

"I can't tell my kids he's dead," I say. "We'd have to have a funeral."

"We've already decided, divorced, not dead," Helena says. "If Bert is missing, we'll once again be suspects. The best thing to do is pretend he's alive, quietly divorce him, and then have him move away."

"He can't just drop out of my kids' lives without a word!" I protest.

"We'll figure it out," Helena says, downing another glass of whiskey. "I don't want my daughter to need years of therapy because of Robert any more than you do."

"We're all gonna shneed therapy," Crystal slurs. "And aura cleansings."

"Oh please, he lied to you for a few months," Helena isn't slurring, but I notice she keeps blinking at Crystal like she can't quite keep her in focus. "He lied to me for years."

"And I guess I'm the biggest moron of all," I jump in, staring down at my empty glass and wondering how it got that way. "I thought I was the only woman for him...I thought that we were each other's everything." I actually start to cry then. Because the truth is, I miss him already. I miss the Bert I thought I'd married. I refill my glass of whiskey, drain it, and then take another. I don't know why I thought this stuff tasted bad. It's yummy once you get used to the bite.

"Look, I'll figure out a way to sort it all out," Helena announces. "Get us all divorced. Who knows how he even did it, or if his marriage to discount wiccan barbie over here is even valid."

"I have the paper," Crystal tells us. "Do you think I can just return the receipt and get ush divorced?"

"That's not how a marriage license works," Helena tells her. Her tone adds a silent, *idiot.*

"Hey, I may not have kids or a years-long relationship with Bobby, but he's the man I married. And I loved him." Her face goes dark. "I was his wife, too."

"Look, his body is disposed of," Helena's voice remains confident despite her body listing to the side. "As long as we can keep the sham going for our kids, it will be fine. We'll just have him fade out and eventually, poof. He'll be gone."

"How are we going to trick the kids?" I ask, because this is the part that really worries me. They would be devastated to learn their father was dead, but I think it would be even more hurtful if he just disappeared and never contacted them again.

Helena eyes me. "Magic."

Despite years of selling objects with magic qualities, I've never been tempted to use them myself. It's always felt like playing with fire.

And now we've all been burnt.

"Do you guys feel any different?" I ask. We'd experienced something, that's for sure. And it was full of raw power. But now I just feel like normal me. Tired and sad.

"You mean from what happened with the *talentum*?" Crystal asks as she pours the last bit of whiskey, splitting it between our three glasses.

"Something happened," Helena says waving her hand erratically as if trying to wipe away what happened at the wharf. "Each of us bled on the *talentum*, which probably set it off, and we had that odd flying moment, but we probably needed to chant or perform an invocation to seal the deal. But we didn't, so it shouldn't be binding. The contract is null and void."

Crystal squints at Helena. "That's not quite how magic works, but I think you're right. If it was permanent we'd know by now."

I sigh and settle my head, which feels oddly heavy, into my hand. This at least is a relief. "You know," Helena says into the sudden pause. "You *could* be pregnant," she stabs a finger in Crystal's direction.

"What?" Crystal asks, horrified.

"Don't tell me that you didn't have sex on your dirty weekend," Helena accuses.

"It was my fortieth birthday celebration," she clarifies.

"It's your birthday today?" I ask.

"Not anymore, it's after midnight."

"How romantic," Helena mocks. "But my point is still valid. You probably had tons of sex and now you have a late life bun in the oven, you geriatric homewrecker."

I giggle, even though I'm older than Crystal.

"You wrecked Maddie's home first," Crystal fires back. "And what's been in my vagina is none of your business," she says, reddening. "But I'm not a dumb kid who would accidentally become pregnant. Give me some credit."

That feels like an insult to me, but I know she doesn't mean it that way. "Whatever. It's not like sex with Bert was earth-shaking," I say with a laugh. I'm feeling warm and floaty and this booth is so cushy I might just lie down right here.

Both women stare at me, eyebrows raised. "You two must know," I say, thinking we'd all have the same story. "Sex with

Bert is just...okay. We mostly stick to missionary and it often feels a bit...rote. Or like a chore no different than doing the dishes or folding socks." I titter, hoping they'll join in.

I thought the other wives would back me up, but instead I see the shock and pity in Helena and Crystal's eyes. I close my heavy eyes, not wanting to look at it.

In an overly loud whisper, I hear Crystal say to Helena, "I probably ssshouldn't tell her that sex with Bobby was more than just earth-shaking, we had a spiritual connection."

"No," Helena answers. "And you shouldn't tell me either." Then as if she can't help herself she adds, "and there's no way you had better sex with Robert than I did. I have never been more sexually compatible with another person in my life."

"Bobby and I—HIC—were gonna take a trip to a clothing—HIC—optional—HIC—resort," Crystal replies in between a bout of hiccups. "He said—HIC—I made him feel—HIC—free."

Helena slams her hand down on the table, a competitive light making her eyes burn in a rather scary way. "There's no way Robert and you had what he and I did."

"We had tantric sex!" Crystal cries out loud enough for the entire room to hear him.

Not to be outdone, Helena begins to list her own sexual exploits. "We once emptied out a sex shop! Costumes! Toys! Bondage ropes! A sex swing! And it wasn't just a bunch of gag gifts we stuffed in a drawer. There's a whole room in my basement. I hired a handyman to install the sex swing. And we used it! A LOT!"

I'm pretty sure everyone left in this place is staring at us, but I am keeping my eyes determinedly squeezed closed. I don't know why I can still hear them, though. All at once it's too much for me.

"ENOUGH!" I say, slamming my hands on the table. I stare at the two women who seemed to have multiplied while my eyes were shut. There are now at least three of each of them.

"This is not a competition! And if it was, I'd win, because Bert and I were married for twenty-five freaking years! And we were happy!" I fumble in my purse for my phone and with clumsy fingers eventually manage to turn it on and open it to my Instagram page. "LOOK!" I demand. "This is our lives. No filter!" I pause and then admit, "Well, some filters, but that doesn't mean it wasn't real." I gulp, hearing my own words. A sob bubbles up and escapes. More quickly follow.

Crystal silently hands me a tissue.

She and Helena stare back at me helplessly.

"Was it real? Was any of it?" I ask. There's not really anything else to say after that and we decide to call it a night.

I take a rideshare home after we agree to stay in touch about what do with our totally dead—but pretending he's not—husband. So for now we're "friends" in the same way my gynecologist who follows my Instagram account is: it's weird and a little uncomfortable, but I can live with it.

The whole way home I try not to think about Crystal's tantric sex flex and Helena's pleasure room in her basement. But it goes round and round in my head until I have to ask the driver to pull over so I can puke onto the side of the road.

After that all I want to do once I get home is fall into bed and forget this night ever happened. I climb the steps up to my room, while my head swims. I take a second, grateful that Ollie is at his grandparents' house. Tonight Bert and I were supposed to go to a hotel after the vow renewal. I would be so ashamed to have Ollie see me this way.

It's a struggle to get ready for bed but I know that I don't want to wake up with crusty vomit breath and last night's clothes, so I take the time to down some water and ibuprofen, brush my teeth, and pull on my favorite pair of flannel pajamas even if they aren't really appropriate for a warm August night.

I slide beneath the covers on my side of the bed, trying my hardest not to think about how he'll never again warm his side of the bed, when suddenly I hear him say,

"Babe, thank god you're finally home."

"AUUUGHHH!" I scream loud enough to wake the dead, or to scare the already woken dead because Bert screams right back at me.

"Ah, Maddie! You'll give me a heart attack!"

"You can't have a heart attack. You're dead!" Just to make sure, I reach out to touch him. My hand goes right through.

He looks down sadly, watching as my fingers pass through his chest.

"Right, I keep forgetting," he says with his usual charming shrug, the one I've always found irresistible. But not anymore.

"No," I say, pointing a finger at him. "This time I am not forgiving you."

"All right, but Maddie, let me explain."

"Explain?" I laugh hysterically. "Okay, how about we start with this. Why did we have bad sex?"

"What?" Bert stares at me and I realize this is not the question he expected. Honestly, it wasn't where I meant to start either, but for whatever reasons right now it feels like the most pressing.

"You heard. Now answer me."

"Are you drunk?"

"You're drunk!" I shout at him, totally more drunk than I've ever been before in my life. "And you're a cheater and a liar. And also you're dead."

I go to the bathroom, needing another drink of water after that scream tore through my throat.

"Baby, you mean the most to me. That's why I'm here." I sip the cold water and let him continue. "Those women mean nothing to me."

"And the child you have with Helena? The one who is only a few months older than Ollie?" I ask. He has no words to explain. "And..." I continue. "All the sex? Why didn't you rock my world? I've only ever had sex with you, Bert," I tell him. "I thought the way we did it was how it was. Sure, sometimes I wondered if there was more, but I never even thought of cheating. I was always ALWAYS loyal to you. Why wasn't that enough?"

His answer, much like his performance in our marriage bed, is not satisfying. "Maddie, you're beautiful, but you're not...sexy. you're the mother of my children, well, most of them. I just...don't see you as a sexual being. You're too buttoned up."

"Helena is buttoned up and you did sex swing stuff with her!"

Bert winces. "She told you about that, huh?" And then as if he can't help himself, he sighs. "Wish we could have had more time."

I throw the glass at his head. It goes right through and shatters against the wall.

"Sorry, sorry. Maddie, I'm trying to be honest here. Helena is buttoned up in a way that makes you want to rip her shirt open and ruffle her feathers. You're buttoned up in a way that makes me think of freshly baked cookies and hot cocoa. And you know I love freshly baked cookies with cocoa!"

"Love them, sure," I snarl. "But you don't want to—" The f word almost comes out of my mouth. But that's not who I am. "You know what them," I finally finish.

Bert smiles at me fondly. "This is what I'm talking about, Mads. You can't even say the f word, much less do it. We made tender love and it was sweet every time. But to do anything else never even occurred to me. Even before the kids arrived, when we were basically just kids, you were always so mom-ish."

And then he says the most hurtful words I'll ever hear, "Most women are a cocktail in bed. Helena was Grey Goose Vodka, classy with a kick. Crystal was kombucha mixed with moonshine—homemade and a little crazy. But you, Maddie darling, you were a glass of warm milk on a cold night."

The blood drains from my face and I almost barf. Maybe Bert's right. Maybe I am just a sexless woman. The type of person you have sex with in the dark with your socks on.

I throw my glass at him, but it sails through his apparition and shatters on the bathroom wall. "Ef you Bert," I tell him.

I march into the bedroom, wanting him to follow, wanting us to keep fighting. Wanting him to somehow say something that will comfort me. But there's nothing Bert could say to ever make this okay.

———

Get more of Maddie's story! Powers of the Zodiac Book 1: The Midlife Gemini's Guide to a Bad Horoscope - is available wherever books are sold!

ALSO BY THE AUTHORS

See the Mythverse through different eyes with the complete seven book series...

GRAVE NEW WORLD:

Down & Dirty Supernatural Cleaning Services

Book 1

Sometimes you have to play dirty.

I'm Paige Harper and I clean up supernatural messes. But my personal life is something I can't seem to straighten out.

I accidentally married a fae, and even though we've been divorced for years, Jax still manages to land me in hot water. Like, putting my house on the table at a high stakes poker game type of hot.

Now, he's been arrested for murder and the cops want to pin a series of vampire killings on him. I don't know if he did it or not. But I do know he needs to be at that poker game or else my house is gone.

In order to get Jax out, I turn to Nico, a one-eyed werewolf private detective, for help. Nico is a handsome, dangerous, ladies man and I have no intention of falling prey to his charms.

Although, that's easier said than done as the two of us begin crawling through the dirty underbelly of the supernatural world...

It's a good thing I brought my broom.

Grave New World is the first book in an all new paranormal mystery series filled with laughs and romance!

————

Supes were once just a myth. That's where Edie's story starts. But by the end of it...she'll have changed the whole world.

Read Fire & Flood: Mythverse Book 1 ebook for FREE! You can find it wherever books are sold!

At Mount Olympus Academy, a little learning is a dangerous thing...

Revenge. That's why I decided to join the assassination class at Mount Olympus Academy. A monster killed my father and grandmother - and I'm going to make them pay.

But first I have to learn how.

I'm Edie. Once I was just a normal girl with asthma and a bad back. Now, though, I'm at a school taught by Greek gods. My classmates are vampires, witches, and shifters. We're all training to fight in the war between the gods and monsters.

There's also...Val. He's a vampire, but he's different from the others. Plus, he's got secrets too.

I get secrets. The wings that sprout from my back were hidden from me my entire life. I also sometimes breathe fire. But no one - including me - can figure out what I fully shift into. Honestly...a part of me doesn't want to know.

But if I'm going to avenge my family, I need to figure it out before I flunk out.

Read Fire & Flood on ebook for FREE! You can find it wherever books are sold!

DOWN & DIRTY SNEAK PEEK

Chapter 1

Cleaning up after a vampire rave sucks.

Pun intended.

My first one, I came armed with a whole truckload of hydrogen peroxide, expecting blood stains everywhere. In my mind, they covered the walls and floors and ceilings. I expected something like what a plasma donation center would look like if it was run by someone hopped up on way too much Mountain Dew.

It turns out, though, that vampires are not messy eaters. You might even say they don't like to waste a single drop of their meal. It's sacred to them the way Ho-Ho's were to my seventh-grade math teacher.

So yeah, it's not the prospect of scrubbing away blood stains that's getting me down as I drive through the warehouse district searching each building for the 6669 the vamps paint on the wall of their chosen party spot. The number's some sort of vampire humor, I think. Or maybe not. They're hard to read and I'm not interested in getting close enough to find out anything about them beyond that they pay in cash.

"Where is this stupid place?" I ask aloud, even though there's no one else in the van with me. Although...my van is kind of sentient. Like a cross between Christine and Herbie, it's both terrifying and adorable.

Vanna was stolen ages ago. Back when she...er, *it*, was just a normal Grand Caravan with stained seats and a dented back fender from some tailgating asshole. I figured that was the last I'd see of it, but a few months back I opened my door and there was Vanna (yes, I named her and yes I hate myself for it). The same...but also totally different.

I would've sent her straight back to the impound lot where she was found if it wasn't for the fact that I was desperate for transportation. The transmission had just died on my previous van and without wheels I had no job. So I used Vanna, figuring I could just pretend she was normal. Just another vehicle.

That didn't last long.

In response to my question, Vanna takes over steering, which is always annoying. But I forgive her as she parks us in front of a building, the 6669 on the wall straight ahead.

From the outside the warehouse looks totally unremarkable. Just another big boxy building. I can't hold back a big sigh as I grasp the handles on the giant sliding door. Putting all my weight into it, I pull the door hard. With a groan it gives way, gliding open and allowing a bright shaft of sunlight to cut through the dark interior.

"Aw fuck," I say as a giant water tank fills my vision. I'm not talking about some little pet store thing; this is Sea World size. I have no idea how I'm gonna drain this thing and scrub it spotless. That's the job, though. I'm supposed to leave only the dust motes and a sparkling clean tank behind when I'm done.

This alone would be a monumental task, but as I walk into the warehouse and closer to the tank and the moving shadows within, I know it's gonna get worse.

And it does.

Sharks. Big ones, too. They glide through the water with silent menace.

Those asshole vamps decided to have an underwater rave and feed on fucking sharks.

I thought the lions were the worst. Before that, I thought the pigs were the worst.

Clearly, I was wrong all those times. Because really, vampires are the worst. Always and forever—they are The. Worst.

I take a minute to swear viciously and creatively, cursing not just vampires but all the paranormal creatures that decided to come out of hiding a decade ago and totally screw up everything. Sometimes I hear people say that it's better to know than to live in ignorance. I disagree. The time when I believed that werewolves, harpies, and faeries were all just stories was a great time. An easier, simpler one too.

I was only in my early twenties when everything changed. My dad's cleaning business was struggling and I'd just graduated with a degree in English that I was quickly realizing was pretty much useless in the real world. Then we had a little apocalypse. Cities disappeared beneath the sea. Crops failed. And all the supes came out to play. Suddenly college degrees didn't mean much. Survival was our entire focus.

I got married to my boyfriend, 'cause it felt like we might all die and I guess I wanted to wear a white dress first? I don't know. It wasn't the greatest decision. I also went into business with Dad. But we revamped it. Pun intended.

Harper Cleaning became Down & Dirty: Supernatural Cleaning Services. Dad said we were kinda like the clean-up crew for the Ghostbusters. "Think about it," he'd say. "Someone had to mop up that marshmallow mess, and I bet they got paid good money. Hazard pay, right?"

He was right. The business thrived. My marriage failed. But overall, life was good.

Until my parents disappeared along with a few hundred thousand other folks.

But that's another story.

Right now, I gotta figure out how to get these sharks outta this tank.

Luckily, we're in the Newark Port district. I understand now why they chose this location. But still, the Bay is a good ten minutes away. Can a shark survive that long out of water?

Pulling out my phone, I start to Google.

Some people might think I'm just a cleaning lady, but in truth, this job requires way more than just a mop and broom.

Yesterday I was choking on feathers cleaning out a frat house that had been full of chicken shifter strippers. Today I'm wrestling sharks. Tomorrow I might be scrubbing harpy droppings off some vocal Humans First protester's roof and lawn.

Down & Dirty is more than just a job. It's a lifestyle.

GRAVE NEW WORLD: Down & Dirty Supernatural Cleaning Services Book 1 is available now! Start this 7 book series today!

FIRE & FLOOD SNEAK PEEK

Chapter One

My parents and sister are at the airport, getting ready to board a plane headed toward Greece. Meanwhile, I'm waiting to be checked out of the hospital.

I'm supposed to be on that flight with them—a three-month work trip that my archeologist mom organized. But two weeks earlier I came down with a virus that turned into pneumonia. This, combined with my lifelong mortal enemy, asthma, made breathing suddenly a lot harder. And then nearly impossible.

That's where the hospital comes in.

The doctors saved my life. And then totally ruined it by telling my parents I should stay home tucked under a blanket on my grandmother's couch so I could be all rested up for my senior year of high school come fall.

I honestly didn't think they would really go without me. No offense to my grandma, but she's pretty old and kinda wobbly. No way would my parents leave their sickly daughter with her while they were on a totally different continent.

"Leave me behind? Screw that," I'd laughed right after the doctor who gave me the bad news left the room.

No one else laughed. Mom, Dad, and my older sister Mavis just stared back at me.

I swallowed, not liking those looks. "Right?"

"Well, sweetheart—" Mom paused as. she took off her glasses and began to clean them on the hem of her shirt. It's one of her favorite avoidance tactics. When I was ten and asked her what sex was, she polished so long and hard that she snapped them in half.

Suddenly I was worried.

"Dad?" I turned to my no-bullshit go-to guy.

"Sweetheart, we rented out our house. Not to mention that for Mom, it's a work trip."

"And I'm getting college credits for an internship," Mavis added. That one really stung. Mavis and I have always been close. Sure there's the usual sisterly bickering, but beneath that we genuinely like each other. I was looking forward to spending the summer together exploring Greece with her and hearing about her first year of college out in California. All year she only came home for Christmas and I missed her like crazy. But now she's heading off again. Without me.

I argued—eloquently, I believe, or as eloquently as someone who has to suck on an inhaler when they get too worked up—for my right to go on this trip. Sure, it was about having fun, but it was also about education, and opportunity and... and the fact that I'd already rubbed it in all my ex-friends' faces that I was going.

In the end, we compromised. And by compromised I mean they just decided.

They would go to Greece as planned.

I would stay with Grandma and she would teach me how to knit. Which was also, Mom pointed out, a learning opportunity. They presented me with a big cotton bag filled with a rainbow's worth of yarn and my very own pair of knitting needles.

It was one hell of a consolation prize. But I wasn't raised to be a sore loser, so I forced a smile and a thank you. Somehow I even managed to wish them well on their travels. Did an evil voice deep inside wish them months of chronic diarrhea? Maybe. But at least I didn't say it aloud.

Maybe I can knit them some diapers.

Now, I hold my bag of knitting supplies as a nurse wheels me out to the curb where my grandma waits behind the wheel of her '85 Lincoln. As I settle myself in the passenger seat my phone bings with a text.

MAVIS: We just boarded.

MAVIS: Didn't get seats together, but luckily I've already made friends.

A pic follows this second text. Mavis and some unbelievably good-looking guy grinning into the camera.

That is so typical Mavis. Even her bad luck turns out good. Stuck by herself and ends up next to one of the hottest guys in the universe.

The car jerks sideways and thumps up onto the curb and then down again. My phone flies out of my hand.

"Almost got that sonofabitch!" Grandma yells, giving her steering wheel a slap that I can't decide is meant to be congratulatory or an admonishment. I look back to see an alligator sunning himself beside the ditch at the side of the road. Gran hates them ever since they ate her Bichon Frise, Elsa, and attempts to mow them down with her car whenever possible. "Next time, next time," she mutters.

"Hey Grandma," I say, in my best poor pathetic left behind tone of voice. "Maybe I can drive the rest of the way home? Get some practice in? It would really lift my spirits."

Grandma shoots me a look that is clearly meant to convey she may be seventy-three, but she ain't senile yet. "Sweetheart, you've failed that driving test what is it...eight times now? Didn't the last tester beg you to quit before you killed someone?"

"Grandma, I know how to drive," I protest. "I'm just a bad test taker."

I'm actually epically terrible. I tend to freeze up in high stress situations. And there is no situation more stressful than trying to go where you want without having to beg Mom or Dad for a lift.

"You're sick, Edie. What kind of grandma do you think I am? Why not rest a little bit on the way home? You look a little peaked." The light changes and Grandma floors it, slamming me back into my seat.

Another battle lost. It's true, though, I am tired. I close my eyes and try to pretend I'm on a plane. It's lifting up into the sky, to travel across an ocean, before finally settling down in the land where gods were born.

As we pull into the parking lot behind Grandma's condo the typical Florida afternoon downpour begins. Grandma slowly totters along while holding her little old lady umbrella that she always keeps in her handbag over my head so I don't get soaked and end up back in the hospital. It's nice and all, but I'm about three feet taller than Grandma so I end up just kind of walking hunched over to get under the umbrella, which doesn't make my chest feel too hot.

Finally we get into the creaky old elevator. It grumbles and lurches its way up to the sixth floor. By the time Grandma unlocks the door all I want to do is cry.

"What's that face for?" Dad asks.

I gasp. He's seated at Grandma's breakfast bar with a cup of coffee. Not on a plane to Greece—but here.

"You stayed!" I rush forward, throwing my arms around him. "I knew you wouldn't leave without me. Where are Mom and Mavis? Are they mad they missed their trip?"

The look on Dad's face as he peels away from me tells me everything I need to know. "Edie, it was Mom's grant. And her dream. You know that. Asking her to miss this chance…"

I swallow hard. Force a nod. "Right. I know."

And I do know. Mom met Dad when they were both studying abroad in Greece years ago. They fell in love, she got pregnant, and Mom decided to stay home with us kids and give up her career until we were older. I never really understood it. Why couldn't she do both?

When I ask Mom she'll only says she was overly worried about our safety just like any young mom. Really, though, Dad's always been the more overprotective one, while Mom is constantly pushing me to let go and embrace my wild side. I've tried to tell her I don't have a wild side, that I'm pretty sure I was born without one. That's when she gets this glint in her eye and insists that someday I'm going to surprise myself. If Mavis is around she always like to add, "In bed." Ha ha ha, Mavis.

Anyway, once I started high school, Mom decided it was time to pick up where she left off. She finished her degree and then this opportunity to work in Greece came up. Dad didn't like it. They tried to hide the fact they were arguing, but even though neither of them are screamers, there's always a certain tone to their voices when they're upset. Eventually Mom won and well, it was immediately obvious how excited she was. Suddenly Greece this and Greece that was all Mom could talk about.

So yeah, unless I was on my deathbed, there's no way Mom wasn't getting on that airplane. And Mavis, well, she was always Mom's favorite, while I've always been Dad's.

I hug Dad again. "Thank you for coming back for me."

He ruffles my hair. Or tries. It's wet, so he just sort of rubs my head instead. "Well, I had to decide who needed more help staying out of trouble—you or your mom. You won, but only just barely."

"Hey, Dad," I smile up at him. "Speaking of trouble... since we're here all summer with nothing to do, maybe you can help me get more driving practice in."

"Aw, baby girl." Dad smiles fondly. "I would rather spend an afternoon wrestling alligators than be inside a vehicle you're driving."

"Dad!"

"But I did have an idea." He rummages in his pocket and then holds up two laminated cards with a ta-da expression.

"Those are bus passes."

"Yup. Good all summer. I figured, well, maybe we could explore the public transportation system in our fair city. It's eco-friendly and it'll be an adventure!"

I stare at Dad. He is working so hard to sell this. Only the vice principal of a junior high school would be this excited about bus passes, and only a monster would burst his bubble.

"Wow. Bus passes and knitting. Best summer ever."

Somehow I manage to keep most of the sarcasm out of my voice.

Dad grins back at me. "Best summer ever," he echoes.

Thing is, I think he means it.

———

Read the rest of the Fire & Flood ebook for FREE! You can find it wherever books are sold!

ABOUT THE AUTHORS

Demitria Lunetta is the author of the YA books THE FADE, BAD BLOOD, and the sci-fi duology, IN THE AFTER and IN THE END. She is also an editor and contributing author for the YA anthology, AMONG THE SHADOWS: 13 STORIES OF DARKNESS & LIGHT. Find her at www.demitrialunetta.com for news on upcoming projects and releases.

Kate Karyus Quinn is an avid reader and menthol chapstick addict with a BFA in theater and an MFA in film and television production. She lives in Buffalo, New York with her husband, three children, and one enormous dog. She has three young adult novels published with HarperTeen: ANOTHER LITTLE PIECE, (DON'T YOU) FORGET ABOUT ME, AND DOWN WITH THE SHINE. She also recently released her first adult novel, THE SHOW MUST GO ON, a romantic comedy. Find out more at www.katekaryusquinn.com

Marley Lynn is a lost child of the gods, who waits on the shores of Lake Erie for her parents to bring her home. In the meantime, she contents herself with reading, writing, and gardening. Find out more at www.MarleyLynn.com

facebook.com/MarleyLynnAuthor

ACKNOWLEDGMENTS

Thank you to Marin McGinnis for taking care of our copy edits!

And, of course, a big thank you to our families for putting up with us crazy writers.